DARK CANYON

DARK CANYON

LOUIS L'AMOUR

BANTAM BOOKS
TORONTO · NEW YORK · LONDON · SYDNEY

DARK CANYON
A Bantam Book

Bantam paperback edition / November 1963
Louis L'Amour Hardcover Collection / June 1983

All rights reserved.
Copyright © 1963 by Bantam Books, Inc.

Book designed by Renée Gelman.

If you would be interested in receiving bookends for The Louis L'Amour Collection, please write to this address for information:

> *The Louis L'Amour Collection*
> *Bantam Books*
> *P.O. Box 956*
> *Hicksville, New York 11802*

ISBN 0-553-06241-7
Library of Congress Catalog Card Number: 63:19055

Published simultaneously in the United States and Canada

Bantam Books are published by Bantam Books, Inc. Its trademark, consisting of the words "Bantam Books" and the portrayal of a rooster, is Registered in U.S. Patent and Trademark Office and in other countries. Marca Registrada. Bantam Books, Inc., 666 Fifth Avenue, New York, New York 10103.

PRINTED IN THE UNITED STATES OF AMERICA

0   9   8   7   6   5   4   3   2

To Catherine . . .

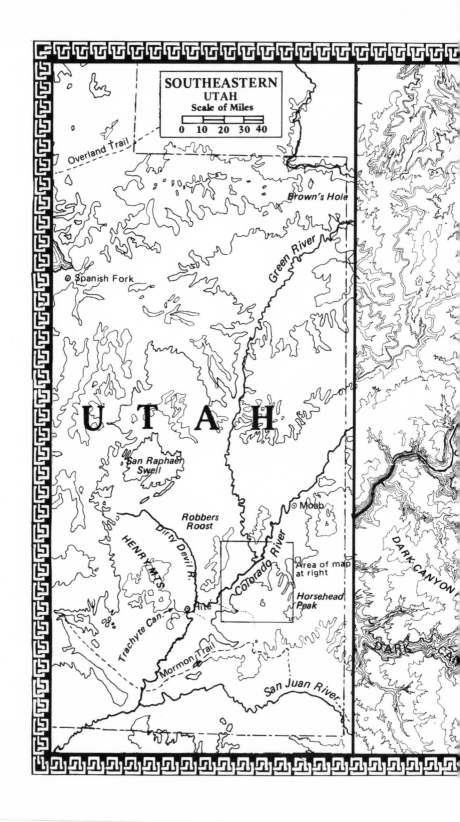

SOUTHEASTERN
UTAH
Scale of Miles

0   10   20   30   40

Overland Trail

Brown's Hole

Green River

Spanish Fork

U T A H

San Raphael
Swell

Robbers
Roost

Moab

Dirty Devil R.

Colorado River

Area of map
at right

Horsehead
Peak

HENRY MTS.

Hite

Trachyte Can.

Mormon Trail

San Juan River

DARK CANYON

DARK CAN

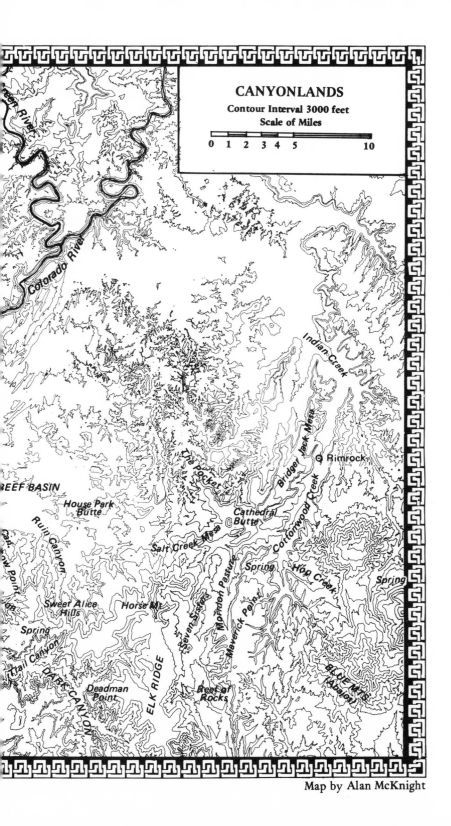

CANYONLANDS
Contour Interval 3000 feet
Scale of Miles
0 1 2 3 4 5 10

Map by Alan McKnight

ONE

When Jim Colburn rode into the hide-out at sundown he was not alone. There was a gangling youngster riding with him, a kid with narrow hips and wide, meatless shoulders and chest. The old Navy .44 looked too big for him, despite his height.

Jim Colburn stepped down from the saddle and looked around at Kehoe, Weaver, and Parrish. He was a tough man with no nonsense about him, and he was their acknowledged leader.

"This here is Gaylord Riley," he said. "He's riding with us."

Parrish was stirring beans, and he merely glanced up and offered no comment. Weaver started to object, but at the expression in Colburn's eyes he decided against it; but he was angry. From the beginning there had just been the four of them, no outsiders invited. What they had to do they did with four men, or they left it alone. Kehoe dropped his cigarette and toed it into the sand. "Hoddy, boy," he said.

They ate in silence, but when they had finished eating the kid moved over and helped Parrish clean up. Nobody said anything until Colburn had one boot off and was rubbing his foot, then it was he who spoke.

1

"I got myself in a corner. He pulled me out of it."

At daybreak they moved out, taking the trail warily at first. Four hard-bitten, veteran outlaws and a lean, raw-boned kid on a crow-bait buckskin. Kehoe was lank and lazy-seeming, Parrish stocky and silent, while Weaver was a brusque man, and this morning an angry one. Jim Colburn, their leader in all things, was a good man with a gun. So were they all.

Weaver's irritation at the stranger's presence was obvious, but nothing was said until they paused at the stream on the outskirts of town.

"We'll handle it the same as always," Colburn said. "Parrish with the horses, Weaver and Kehoe with me."

Weaver did not even turn his head. "What does *he* do?"

"He'll ride to that big cottonwood and dismount. He will stand right there until we come by, and if there's shooting, he'll cover us."

"That'll take nerve."

Gaylord Riley looked at Weaver. "That's what I got," he said.

Weaver ignored him. "You ain't never been wrong yet, Jim," he said, and they rode on into town.

Riley dismounted and was busy with his cinch, standing behind his horse with a clear view of the street. The bank was two hundred yards off, and the street was empty and the hour early.

When Colburn, Weaver, and Kehoe came out of the bank and stepped into their saddles the street was still empty.

They had covered almost half the distance to the spot where Gaylord Riley waited, when the banker ran from the bank shouting. He carried a rifle, and he swung it up to fire.

Gaylord Riley had his choice and took it. He aimed at the hitch-rail in front of the banker. Splinters flew at his shot, and the banker leaped wildly for the shelter of the doorway.

The gang rode by the kid and he sprang to the saddle and rode off after them just as people rushed into the street.

In the arguments in the town afterward, some said there were three outlaws, some four. Nobody appeared to have noticed the man farther up the street. Had they observed him, they might have suspected him of trying to run down the outlaws.

They rode hard for the first mile, trying for as much distance as possible. Then the kid saw a dozen steers feeding in the grass close by the trail and, cutting out, he drove them in behind the four outlaws, blotting out their tracks.

Something over a mile farther on they came upon a stream and abandoned the cattle, riding upstream in the ankle-deep water. They were able to follow the stream for half a mile and then they left it and turned into the hills. The pursuit never found their trail, never even came close.

Their take was small, and Weaver showed his irritation when an equal share was counted out for Riley.

Kehoe dropped his share into a pocket. "You could have killed that banker," he commented.

"There was no need."

The four had been together a long time. They had hunted buffalo together on the Staked Plains of west Texas, and together they had punched cows for Shanghai Pierce, Gabe Slaughter, and Goodnight. Their first step over the line that divides the law-abiding from the lawless was over a matter of wages due them.

Tobe Weston had a handy way with a pen, and a couple of times he saved himself a few dollars by outfiguring his hands, who were notoriously casual about money. The few dollars whetted his appetite until he managed to short every hand who worked for him except Deuces Conron, his strong right arm.

Here and there some cowhand who paid more attention to figures than others would object. When they could not be outtalked they could always be outgunned, and Weston's greed grew with success.

When Colburn, Kehoe, Weaver, and Parrish came to work for him they had heard none of the stories, and it was four months before they did. They decided at once to quit.

Tobe Weston shorted them two months each, and when they objected Deuces was there to back him up. Kehoe was prepared to argue, as were the others, but not to accept the challenge of the four shotguns peering over window sills at them—shotguns in the hands of Weston's family.

"Forget it," Colburn advised, and they rode away.

They hid out in the mountains and waited for three weeks, and when Tobe Weston rode to town in his black suit they knew their time had come. He was on his way back when they came down out of the rocks and met him and collected their due. Only at the last minute they decided it would serve Weston right if they took all he had. And they did.

That had been the beginning. And that had been a good many years ago.

Their strength lay in careful planning, and in their closeness to each other. They did not talk, and they did not separate; and they would have no strangers in their group until Colburn came back with Gaylord Riley.

The Black Canyon stage holdup was typical of their work, and it took place only three weeks after the kid joined them.

That stage had been held up so many times the drivers were accustomed to it and knew all the likely places. Only Jim Colburn did it in another way. He held up the stage out on the open flat, in the area with the least cover, and where a holdup was unlikely.

The driver saw the buckboard coming along the trail, and it was in plain sight for over a mile, coming along at a trot, trailing a little dust. When it drew near the driver saw that a lean, gangling kid in a farmer's straw hat was driving, with an old man huddled in a blanket beside him on the seat. The kid had one arm around the old man as if to steady him on the seat.

As the stage drew near, slowing to pass the buckboard, the old man raised a feeble hand to signal them to stop.

They did stop, and the tall boy helped the old man down from the buckboard. One of the passengers got down to help, and from under the blanket the old man produced a six-shooter.

From the back of the buckboard, two more men rolled out from under a canvas tarp, and the Black Canyon stage had been held up once again. Afterward at least two of the people on the stage were sure the boy had himself been a prisoner. He certainly, with that buckboard and hat, could be no outlaw. And he had seemed to be frightened. Or so they thought.

Riley helped around camp, and talked little, but his presence continued to irritate Weaver. Loafing on the street at Bradshaw, studying the bank there, Weaver said suddenly to Kehoe, "I've had about enough of that kid. What did Jim ever bring him along for?"

"He ain't a bad kid. Leave him alone."

"Something about him gets on my nerves," Weaver insisted, "and we don't need him."

"Don't brace him," Kehoe advised. "You'd get your tail twisted."

"Huh?" Weaver was contemptuous. "He ain't dry behind the ears yet."

Kehoe brushed the ash from his cigarette. "The kid's a gunfighter."

"Him? For two bits I'd—"

"You'd get killed."

Weaver was angry, but curious, for Kehoe was no fool. He was cannier than most, when it came to that. "What makes you say that?"

"Watch him. Nobody makes a move that he doesn't see, and he never gets that right hand tangled up. When he takes hold of anything it's always with his left. You watch."

Grudgingly, Weaver accepted him. Parrish sometimes rode beside him, but it was only to Colburn or Kehoe that he talked. When they crossed the border to spend what they had taken, Riley bought drinks but did not drink, and he spent little. Weaver was usually broke within a few days, and Parrish almost as soon. None of them was particularly provident.

One morning, three miles south of Nogales, in Sonora, Weaver crawled out of his blankets with a hang-over. Parrish was cooking, Riley was cleaning his rifle. Colburn and Kehoe were not there.

"I took in too much territory," Weaver said. "You got a drink, Parrish?"

Parrish shook his head, but Riley turned to his blanket roll and fished out a bottle. "Hair of the dog," he said, and tossed the bottle to Weaver.

Weaver pulled the cork and drank. "Thanks, kid," he said.

"Keep it," Riley said. "The way you headed into it last night I figured you could use that today."

Later, after Riley had ridden off, Weaver said, "Maybe I got that kid wrong."

"You sure did. He's all right." Parrish handed him a cup of coffee. "He's a good kid."

Weaver took another drink, then corked the bottle and put it away. He seemed to be considering what Parrish had said.

"That's it," he said at last. "That's just the trouble. He's a good kid."

TWO

Colburn was shaving, and there was no one else in camp but Weaver.

"What happened that time, Jim, when you picked up the kid?"

Colburn tilted his head slightly and sighted along his jaw. After he had drawn the razor carefully along he rinsed it in the water. "Poker game," he said, "and they cold-decked me. I caught one of them with an extra card and drew on him . . . and then I saw they had two guns on me. They were all set to let me have it."

Colburn worked with the razor for a few minutes and then went on. "They laughed at me. You can put up your gun and get out, Colburn. We know who you are, and you can't complain to the law."

He lathered his chin again. "That card shark got out his six-shooter, too, and they were boxin' me. I'd no chance the way things shaped up, and whilst I was sure they were a lot of yellow-bellied tinhorns, nobody but a fool calls a hand like they had against me.

"Well, I'd had a drink and I was sore, and I wasn't goin' to take it. Sure, I was a damn fool and they'd have killed me, but I'd have taken them with me—or some of them."

He paused again to shave. After a moment he added, "I told 'em so. I told 'em, 'All right, you've bought it. You pulled iron on me and thought I'd back down. You figure everybody is as yellow-bellied as you are. Well, you're goin' to have to fight.' "

He chuckled. "Oh, they were scared! I seen that! Never for a minute did they think I'd show fight with those odds again' me. And then this kid spoke up.

"There were four, five others in the room and the kid was at the bar. He just spoke up real cool-like, and he'd a gun in his fist, an' he said, 'Deal me in, too, or give him back his money.' "

Colburn shaved, then stropped his razor. "They were sweatin', you can bet on that. For that matter, so was I. Right then I guess I'd become cold sober, because all of a sudden those three guns looked almighty big.

"The thing was, they knew this kid. What they knew I still don't know, but they wanted no part of him, and he was more than likely wishin' a fight with them.

"Then that gambler shoved my money at me. 'Take it. Take it and get out.' And then he said to the kid, 'Riley, you're fixing to get yourself killed.'

"And the kid says, 'How about now?' But nobody taken him up. So when I pulled out, I invited him along. He was foot-loose, and I couldn't turn my back on him after that."

"You sure couldn't." Weaver was quiet for a few minutes. "Jim," he said at last, "you've been patient with me. All this time that kid's been getting at me, and it taken me a while to figure it out. He doesn't belong with us, Jim."

Colburn finished his shaving and cleaned his razor and brush.

Weaver got up and walked around the fire. "Jim, none of us was cut out for outlaws. Not you, not me, nor the others. We were cowhands, and we should have stayed with it. We've robbed up and down the country, and there's been times when I was mighty ashamed of it.

"We've been at it for years, and what have we got? No home, not a piece of ground anywhere we can call our own. On the dodge most of the time, livin' like this. When we get a few dollars we blow it in, and we're back where we started. All right—that's us. But it ain't for this kid.

"He's right where we were fifteen years ago, and if he keeps on he'll be right where we are fifteen years from now, unless he catches lead—and the chances are good.

"Face up to it, Jim. It's gettin' tougher. The telegraph has come west. Not much yet, but it soon will be, and the law is gettin' organized. That kid should get out whilst he can."

Weaver lifted a hand. "Don't say you ain't thought of it. At first I thought you were playin' a favorite, then I could see you were deliberately keepin' the kid from being identified with us . . . at least so's he'd have an argument."

"What have you got in mind?"

"Let me talk to him."

Two days later they were camped on the Sonora in a little grove of cottonwoods and willows, with a scattering of smoke trees farther up the draw.

Weaver was washing a shirt when the kid came down and shucked his own shirt and started washing it. Weaver glanced at the thin brown shoulders. There were three bullet holes in Gaylord Riley's body.

"You've caught some lead," Weaver commented.

"When I was a kid. Maybe a year or so before I left Texas. Pa an' me was livin' on a little two-by-four place down on the Brazos. Pa was gimpy in one leg, caught a bullet fightin' Comanches the time they killed ma. We had ourselves a few cows, and we're makin' out to have more.

"One night some fellers started making a gather of our stock and we fetched up to stop them. They killed pa, and they touched me up some. They figured me for dead.

"I crawled back to the cabin and fixed myself up. I'd this hole here, and one you can't see—in my leg. There was an old Tonkawa lived three, four miles from us, and I got onto a horse and rode over there. When I got well I got pa's old six-gun and went to work.

"That Tonk, he was a tracker, and he located one of those

men for me. The cattle had been driven out of the country, but this man was spendin' money he'd no right to have. I hunted him up."

Weaver worked over his shirt, listening. The story was not unfamiliar. How many times had such things happened on the lawless frontier?

"He was riding that buckskin with pa's brand still on it, and I called him for a thief."

Weaver had seen such things, and a time or two had had his own hand in them. He could see it clearly now, as Riley told his simple, unadorned tale. The thief would have reckoned his chances good against a wet-eared boy.

"There were five of them raided us that night. Two of them I could never find, but there'll come a time. My pa," he said, "was never no hand with a gun. He hunted here and there, but he was a man who wished for no trouble, and he wasn't up to a shoot-out with that outfit that robbed him."

"Are you still hunting those others?"

"Seems to me there's a lot else to do in the world. I'm thinking of my own future some, but I have it in mind that a day will come when we will meet up. Then I'll have my say."

Weaver rinsed out his shirt and hung it in the sun to dry. He squatted back on his heels and lit a cigarette. "Riley," he said, "I've been thinking back. You've got around six thousand dollars stashed away in your outfit."

Gaylord Riley said nothing at all, but Weaver was amused to see the way that right hand stayed clear of the water. The kid was careful, and Weaver liked that. He had never liked a cocky youngster. He liked them sure, careful, and honest.

"Jim is pushing forty. Parrish and me are upwards of thirty-six. Kehoe, he's just thirty-two. We have been outlaws a long time and it hasn't got us a thing, but we ain't going to be anything else until we get too old to ride."

Riley said nothing, and he began to wring out his shirt.

"This life gets you nothing. Jim Colburn's a shrewd and careful man and we've been lucky, but let me tell you—Jim's scared."

"Him? He ain't scared of nothing!"

"Rightly speaking, he isn't scared, but he's scared of the odds. We've been too lucky for too long. All right—we've planned it always, but the thing a man can't figure is the unexpected. You check the time a bank opens and when folks begin to get there. Most people are creatures of habit, so all we have to do is learn those habits. But what about the man who forgets something? He forgot to tell the banker something, or he meant to keep part of the money he deposited. For whatever reason, he goes back.

"Or you stand up a stage out on the road. Nobody is supposed to be around. And then comes an army patrol returning from a scout . . . or maybe there's two or three gun-happy men aboard.

"The thing you can't figure, kid, is the unexpected, and it always happens. Well, we've been lucky, but Jim is scared now, and so am I."

"What's all this talk lead to?"

"You, Riley. Get out of this business."

Weaver reached around and picked up his saddlebags. He dug out his poke and tossed it to Riley. "There's a thousand there. Take it, with what you've got, and buy some cows."

"You're tryin' to get rid of me?"

"Uh-huh." Weaver rubbed his cigarette in the sand until it was carefully put out. "You ain't cut out for it, kid. You don't like to kill, and that's the way it should be. You've been shooting to scare, and that's the best way. Rob a bank, and nobody gives you too much of an argument but the law; but you kill a man, and that man has friends, and they'll chase you to hell. But some day we'll get in a bind and you'll have to kill."

"I'll do what I have to."

"You've killed men, kid, but you were in the right. You kill riding with us, and it's different. It is different in the eyes of the law and of people, and you'll see it different yourself."

"What will Jim say?"

"He likes you . . . like you're his son. We'll all be pleased, Riley. We sure will."

"I can't take your money."

"You ain't taking it. Some day I'll be too stove up to ride, and then I'll come to you and you can fix me up in a shack on your place and let me eat some honest beef."

They walked back to the fire. The way the others looked up, Riley knew they had been waiting for the results of the talk.

Colburn tossed a heavy poke to Riley. "Three thousand there, kid. We're all buying in. You start yourself an outfit."

Gaylord Riley looked down at the poke, and then after a moment he looked up. "This here's fine . . . mighty fine. Always wished a place of my own, like pa wanted."

"One thing, Riley," Colburn advised. "Wherever you settle, you file government claim to your water. You file government claim to all the water you can get. You can take it from me that a range is only as big as its water supply, and when a steer walks too far to water he walks off beef."

Riley picked up the poke. "All right, then."

When he had saddled up, he stepped into the saddle and looked around at them. "You boys take care," he said, "and you remember—there's always a place with me, no matter where I am."

They listened to the sound of his horse's hoofbeats until they died away and the dust settled and lay still. In the stream the water chuckled and rippled over the rocks and among the roots.

Jim Colburn looked around with sudden distaste. "Come on, let's light a shuck," he said.

"I'll miss that kid," Kehoe commented.

"Only four of us again."

Parrish said nothing, but he turned twice to look back.

THREE

When Gaylord Riley was only sixteen he had camped for two nights near a spring at the head of Fable Canyon. They had been still, cold nights in the fall, with stars hanging so low it seemed a man might knock them down with a stick.

Never had he forgotten those magnificent distances, the mountains and canyons, the tremendous reach of unpeopled land, and now he had returned, as he had known he would.

To some the immensity, the solitude, the vastness of sky and landscape would have been appalling, frightening; but to Gaylord Riley, whose nature was attuned to all this, it offered something to the spirit.

Near the head of Fable Canyon, on a bench at the foot of the Sweet Alice Hills, he began the house that would be home. On every side the land fell away, offering an unimpaired view to the north, west, and south. Fifteen miles away as the crow would fly lay the Colorado River, to the north a vast basin of several thousand acres where he planned to run cattle. On the south lay a jumble of canyons, cliffs, and pinnacles that stretched away for a vast distance, to end finally in the Painted Desert.

Long ago this had been an inhabited land, but it was so no

13

longer. Cliff dwellings remained, ruins now, and there were the remains of ancient irrigation. Why the original inhabitants had moved on, no man could guess, but no others had come to fill the gap they left behind, although of late there were stories that the Navajo were beginning to drift into the southern part of the area.

From the moment Gaylord Riley rode away from the outlaw camp he had been thinking of this place. It was not an area anyone else would be likely to think of. There were better grazing lands available, but they were not better for him.

The grazing here was good. There was timber for building, there was an unlimited view, which he liked, good water, and no near neighbors. Moreover, there was a maze of canyons in any direction, so when his friends came to visit they would not need to worry about getting away.

The nearest town was Rimrock, unpeeled and raw, something over twenty miles to the northeast. The town was scarcely a year old, a dusty avenue shaded by cottonwoods and lined by false-fronted stores. It was a one-doctor, no-lawyer, five-saloon town, with two good water-troughs, a deep well, and excellent home-made whiskey.

Nearby were eight prosperous ranches and a pair of lean mining prospects. Local society consisted of the doctor, the banker, the eight ranchers, the preacher, and the newspaper publisher.

It was a town where the leading saloon, as well as one of the smaller ones, was owned by Martin Hardcastle. He was a very large man with a polished, hard-boned face, slicked-down hair, and a handle-bar mustache. Among the regulars at the Hardcastle saloons were Strat Spooner and Nick Valentz.

There were two powers in the town of Rimrock, and in the country around. Martin Hardcastle and Dan Shattuck had been speaking acquaintances, and had often talked together several minutes at a time, either during casual meetings on the street or in Hardcastle's saloon. They did so no longer.

Outwardly there was between them the same reserved amiability as before, but no longer did Shattuck drop into Hardcastle's for his evening drink, or to meet friends. Bit by bit he had withdrawn his trade, transferring it to a saloon across the street. Those who had been inclined to meet Dan Shattuck at Hardcastle's had drifted to the other saloon.

The business was not important to Hardcastle, but Shattuck's attitude was. Hardcastle was sure that Shattuck had not mentioned the reason for his change to any of the others, for their attitudes toward Hardcastle remained the same. Nevertheless, a line had been drawn, sharply and definitely.

Not that the line had not existed before—it had. The trouble was that Martin Hardcastle had overstepped it.

That Sunday afternoon had been warm and bright, and Marie—Shattuck's niece—had been visiting Peg over at Oliver's Boxed O. Dan Shattuck had been working over his ranch books in the room he called his "office." Pico had been braiding a horsehair bridle on a bench in front of the bunkhouse.

Martin Hardcastle had driven into the yard in a spanking new buckboard with a black body and red wheels. He wore a black broadcloth suit and a starched white shirt. Across the front of his vest was a heavy gold chain supporting an elk's tooth.

Pico watched him get down from the buckboard, and he would not have denied his curiosity.

Dan Shattuck answered the door himself. He was a tall, fine-featured man with a shock of graying hair. He was puzzled, and had no idea of what to expect.

Hardcastle was forty-five years old and weighed two hundred and fifty pounds, very little of it fat. He carried himself well, and at times he could be suave and adroit. He was not so now, made abrupt by the very strangeness of what he was about to do.

Seated, he put his big hands on his knees. "Dan," he said abruptly, "I'm a wealthy man. I'm healthy, and I've never been married, but I've decided it's time."

Shattuck had never known Hardcastle except as proprietor of a place where he bought drinks from time to time, or in the meetings natural to two men in a small town. He was even more puzzled when Hardcastle said, "I decided to come to you first."

"Me?"

"Yes, Dan. You see, it's Marie I'm thinkin' of."

Had Hardcastle reached over and slapped him across the face, Shattuck would have been less surprised—and much less angry.

Hardcastle ran a saloon, and to men of Dan Shattuck's stamp and to many others that placed him beyond the pale. A less-known fact was that Hardcastle was also the proprietor of a business operated by three girls in a house by the river. This fact was known to Shattuck, although Hardcastle believed his tracks were well covered.

Dan Shattuck got to his feet abruptly. "You can stop thinking," he said coldly. "When my niece marries it will not be to a saloonkeeper who also trafficks in women. Now get out of here, and if you ever venture to speak to my niece I'll have you publicly horsewhipped and run out of town."

Hardcastle's face had turned red, then white. He started to speak as he reared to his feet. His hands shook, his eyes bulged. Abruptly, he turned and strode from the room, almost stumbling as he went down the steps. He got into his buckboard, whipped it around, and raced toward the road.

Pico put aside his bridle and walked to the house, where Dan Shattuck sat, white-faced and furious. Briefly, he explained to Pico.

"If he so much as makes a move toward her," Pico said, "I shall kill him."

It was only two weeks later that Gaylord Riley rode into Rimrock for the first time. Had Hardcastle been less absorbed in planning a limitation to Dan Shattuck's future he might have paid more attention to the stranger who rode past his saloon and dismounted at the bank.

Strat Spooner did notice. He also noticed the double set of heavy saddlebags Riley took from his horse and carried into the bank.

Amos Burrage looked up from his battered desk at the dusty cowhand.

"I want to make a deposit," Riley said.

Burrage indicated the cashier. "See him," he said.

"I'll see you." Riley lifted his saddlebags to the desk-top. "I want to deposit that, and I want to buy cattle."

Burrage glanced into the saddlebags. There were dozens of small sacks, carefully wrapped. He opened several of them. He saw gold in chunks, in dust, in coins . . . tightly rolled greenbacks.

"That's a lot of money, boy. How'd you come by it?"

Gaylord Riley did not reply, and Burrage felt distinctly uncomfortable under his hard, steady gaze. It irritated him that this young man—he could be scarcely more than twenty—could make him feel as he did.

"The Boxed O has longhorns they might sell," he suggested.

"I want Shorthorns or white-face stock," Riley said.

"The only man around here with white-face cattle is Dan Shattuck, and he won't sell—he went to too much trouble to get them here in the first place. He thinks they will do well here, but nobody else does."

"I do."

"You'll bring in your own, then. Shattuck won't sell. In fact, the Lazy S is in the market for more than they have."

Riley indicated the money. "I'll be drawing against that. Take care of it."

He walked out to the street, a rangy young man in shot-gun chaps, a faded maroon shirt, and a black hat. He paused on the street and gave it his sharp attention while appearing to be beating the dust from his clothes.

With that brief study he located every place in town. He saw Strat Spooner loafing in front of the place called Hardcastle's, saw the buckboard coming down the street driven by a girl, saw the Mexican vaquero who rode beside her.

Riley crossed the street toward the Emporium. He had categorized Spooner in that one brief glance. The man loafing in front of the saloon was probably a hired gunhand or an outlaw. Gaylord Riley had reason to know the type.

Moreover, at a time when any employed cowhand would be

hard at work, this man sat at his ease. He wore brand-new boots that must have cost twice what a cowhand could afford. As Riley crossed the street he was conscious of the man's attention, and knew the reason for it.

Valentz came from the saloon and asked, "Who's he?"

Riley, as he stepped up on the boardwalk in front of the store, heard the question.

The sun lay warm upon the dust of the street, warm upon the buildings, the freshness of their lumber already fading under the sun and wind. Gaylord Riley paused on the walk and looked around again. After all, this would be his town. Here he would come to market, and here he would get his mail—if any.

He frowned, wondering if he could buy a newspaper anywhere in town. And then he saw the sign: *The Rimrock Scout, All the News, Plenty of Opinions.*

Riley strolled down the street and opened the door. The hand press and the fonts of type—these were things of which he knew nothing. The weather-beaten man who walked up to the counter, wiping his hands on a cloth, smiled.

"How are you, son? Huntin' news, or providin' it?"

Riley chuckled. "Figured you might sell me a paper and let me browse through some back issues. Seems to me that's the best way to learn about a community."

The newspaperman thrust out a hand. "Glad to know you're going to be one of us. I'm Sampson McCarty, editor, publisher, and printer. You're the first newcomer who has had sense enough to come in here and find out about the country. You help yourself."

He waved toward a stack of newspapers on a shelf. "That's all there is—thirty-six weeks, thirty-six issues. Take all the time you like, come as often as you like."

"I'm Gaylord Riley. I'm ranching over west."

"That's rough, wild country," McCarty commented. "Not many even ride into that wilderness."

"Suits me. I'll be runnin' cows, not visitin'."

Riley took a handful of newspapers and sat down at a table. He sat where he could look out of the window, his back partly toward McCarty. The newspaper idea was one he had picked up from Jim Colburn. Colburn had discovered that you could get a good idea about how rich a bank was by studying the papers . . . and a good idea about how dangerous the law might be.

McCarty saw at once that there was nothing haphazard about Riley's way of going over a newspaper. The first thing he did was run down the column of box advertisements to check the business and professional ads, making several notes as he went along. Next he scanned the column of local items each issue contained.

McCarty, from his position in setting type, could see over Riley's shoulder, and as he knew every item it was easy to ascertain the reader's interests.

The news story referring to the arrival of Shattuck's Herefords held Riley's attention; but when he came upon the story of Spooner's killing of Bill Banner, he paused to read the item with care. The next story at which he stopped was that of the holdup at Pagosa Springs—or rather, the attempted holdup. Two bandits had been wounded, and one of the outlaws was said to have been a member of the Colburn gang.

He read on, skimming the local items, and at last he pushed back in his chair and was rising when the door opened and Marie Shattuck entered with Pico.

McCarty wiped his hands and came up to the counter again. "How do you do, Marie. Howdy, Pico."

The printer turned and gestured toward Riley. "Miss Shattuck, Pico, meet Gaylord Riley. He's ranching over west. Newcomer."

Riley straightened up, suddenly aware that he was flushing. "Shattuck? Of the Running S?"

"You know of us?"

"Only that you're running Herefords, and I'd like to buy some."

Pico's mahogany face was inscrutable, and he looked at Riley with care. This man had been up the creek and over the mountain—he was no average man.

"Uncle Dan wouldn't dream of selling, Mr. Riley. He had

too much trouble getting them in the first place. But you might talk to him."

When they had paid for their paper and gone, Riley turned to McCarty. "I saw an item there in the paper about a gun battle. Somebody named Spooner. That wouldn't be him sitting down in front of the saloon, would it?"

"It would. And he's a man to leave alone. If you had read back a little further you'd see that two, three months before that one he had another fight . . . killed that man, too."

"Thanks."

McCarty watched him as he left the office and turned down the street; and McCarty, who had operated newspapers or worked as a printer in many western towns, was puzzled.

There were many varieties of men in the West, but this one had none of the diffidence of the average cowhand. Young as he was, he carried himself with a quiet assurance, yet with a watchfulness that reminded McCarty of Earp, Courtright, or Hickok. But he was not one of these, and no other that he had ever heard of.

Rimrock was a town without secrets, and before nightfall McCarty heard the story of the deposit of ten thousand dollars in the local bank. He heard also that Riley had hired two cowhands, both of them known to McCarty.

Cruz was a Mexican, lean, hard-riding, and capable. Darby Lewis was a loafer much of the time, though when he worked he was a top hand on any outfit, but he worked as little as possible.

The restaurant at Rimrock was the town's one attempt at the ways of the city. Instead of merely the usual boarding-house tables, they had a dozen tables that would seat four people each. The boarding-house tables they had as well, and few of the citizens patronized anything else.

Martin Hardcastle ate at one of the smaller tables, and so did Amos Burrage, but there were few others who did except Shattuck and his niece. Gaylord Riley chose a table by himself because he did not wish to be questioned or led into talk. He wanted time to think, to plan, and to sort out what he had learned that day.

Most of all, he wanted to think about what he had read about the attempted robbery at Pagosa Springs, for if the information was true, two of the members of the Colburn gang were wounded, perhaps seriously. If so, they would need food, a hide-out, and maybe medicine.

He sat alone and ate alone, conscious that at a nearby table sat Marie Shattuck, with Pico.

He was sitting where he could watch the door, for he was expecting the sheriff. From the local items he had gathered that Sheriff Larsen ate his supper in the restaurant once or twice each week, and dropped in more often for coffee. Sooner or later they must meet, and Riley preferred it to be now.

Pico glanced at Marie. "New *hombre*," he said slyly.

"Pico! Will you stop trying to marry me off?"

"Your uncle, he is a busy man, and he knows much of cattle, nothing of women. Your mother and your aunt are dead. Who is to look after you if not Pico?"

Suddenly the door opened and Martin Hardcastle came in. Riley, attuned to such things, saw the look he gave Marie, and saw Pico's stiffening; then he saw the Mexican slowly relax, but as a big cat relaxes while watching a snake—quiet, but poised and alert.

Hardcastle glanced at Riley, then walked on to an empty table and sat down, facing Marie. He was within Riley's line of vision, and Riley felt himself stir irritably at the way the big man stared at the girl. She seemed utterly unaware of it, yet Riley was not at all sure of that.

McCarty, who usually ate alone in his own bachelor's shack, decided on this night to invest the price of a meal in the possibilities of news. With a sixth sense given to good newsmen and law officers, he sensed trouble, though without any idea of where it would develop, or how. An ordinarily quiet man who talked little, he was friendly and knew everyone.

He paused as he reached Riley's table. "Had an idea that might help you. If Shattuck won't sell any of his Herefords,

why don't you try the country north of here? I hear some of the
folks coming through on the Overland Trail still have cattle to
sell."

"Sit down," Riley said.

McCarty sat, leaning his forearms on the table. "Sometimes
movers run short of cash and grub, and they'd sell out if you
were there with an offer."

"I may try that."

The door opened again and a man entered and paused,
blinking slowly from small blue eyes almost hidden between
high cheekbones and bushy brows. The bone structure of the
man's face was massive; his hair was blond, mixed with gray.

He was not a tall man, but broad and thick, and he moved
with deceptive slowness. On the vest underneath his coat Riley
could see the gleam of a badge, and he held himself very still.
This was Sheriff Ed Larsen.

Larsen's eyes swept the room, nodding here and there.
Finally his eyes came to rest on Riley, but only for the briefest
instant. They passed over him to McCarty.

"H'lo, Mac," he spoke in a low, deep voice. "You smelling
trouble again?"

McCarty shrugged. "You know I am," he said. "And you can
laugh if you want. It will come."

"I won't laugh. It's headed dis way."

"Trouble?"

"The Colburn gang."

FOUR

Sheriff Ed Larsen turned his slow blue eyes to Riley. "Do you know the Colburn gang?"

"I'm from Texas."

"He's a newcomer, Ed. He's ranching over west of here, and wants to buy some Herefords. I was telling him he might find some among movers along the Overland Trail."

"I t'ink so. Mebbe. Dey are goot cows, dose Hereford." He accepted the coffee the waitress brought to the table and poured a heavy dollop of honey into it. "Rough country west. You t'ink dey do well dere?"

"There's some meadows where I can cut hay for winter feeding, and there's plenty of forage on those high plateaus. And I'm in no hurry. I want to get some good breeding stock and build a good herd."

"Sheep," Larsen said, "dere is money in sheep. More dan in cows, I t'ink."

"I don't know anything about sheep."

Larsen studied Riley thoughtfully. Then he said, "You must know dis country here. It is rough to the west. I t'ink not many know dat country."

"Once—when I was sixteen—I rode through this country. We camped two days at the spring where I've located. I never forgot it."

"Ah? What spring is dat?"

There was no way of avoiding it, so he said, "On a bench of the Sweet Alice Hills—head of Fable Canyon."

Larsen was surprised. The names obviously meant nothing to McCarty, but the old Swede shook his head and muttered, "Dat *is* wild. I t'ink nobody goes dere. And it is high . . . very high oop."

"I like the view."

Larsen nodded. "Yah, I t'ink so. It is a goot view."

Riley was uneasy. The old man was no fool, and if he knew the Sweet Alice Hills he had been over the country more than Riley would have thought, to look at the slow-moving man.

Riley's eyes kept straying to Marie Shattuck, at the table nearby. She was a pretty girl, and there was something about her he liked that had nothing to do with beauty. Twice their eyes met, and Pico had noticed it.

"What, Pico?" Marie teased. "No urging? No seal of approval?"

The Mexican shrugged. "This one I do not know, chiquita, but I would believe he has done much riding. He is no fool, this one."

Riley's mind returned to the Colburn gang. If they had been shot up and some of them wounded they would be desperately in need of help. Moreover, they would need a place to hole up for a while. And the canyons near the ranch offered plenty of places to hide out, and fifty ways in and out of the country—it was one reason he had fastened upon the Sweet Alice Hills.

Larsen droned on, talking of cattle, prices, and forage conditions. Suddenly he glanced sharply at Riley. "You buy some flower seed today, yah? At the store?"

"Yes."

"Goot. It is goot to have flower. I haff roses. You come by some day, I show you. I t'ink a man who plants tree and flower, he come to stay." Larsen got slowly to his feet, and thrust out his hand. "Some flower do well in dis country, some do not. We haff to give dem the chance."

As he walked away, Riley wondered if there was more in that last comment than met the ear? Was Larsen giving him a subtle hint? A hint that he was to have his chance here? Or was that his imagination working overtime?

Of one thing he was sure: the further he could stay away from Larsen, the better.

The following morning he bought three pack horses, all mares. He was packing them with the last of his purchased supplies when he saw a tall, gray-haired man ride into the street. His bay horse wore a Running S brand. This had to be Dan Shattuck.

Gaylord Riley walked into the street to stop him, and Shattuck drew up. "I'm in the market for some white-face cattle," Riley said, "and I understand you have some."

Shattuck nodded. "I have some, but none for sale." His cool blue eyes surveyed Riley. "You're new around here. At present mine are the only white-face cattle around, so if you do ac-quire some I would suggest you run them far from mine. We would not want to have any trouble."

Riley felt anger rise within him, but he said simply, "I shall buy white-face cattle, and I shall run them on the range I have chosen, and if we have any trouble you may be sure I'll know how to handle it."

Abruptly, he turned and strode back to the mares he was packing. Cruz glanced at his face, then at the horseman in the street, who had not moved. "Do not make an enemy of him, amigo," Cruz said quietly. "He is a good man, but a strong-minded one."

"To hell with him!"

Martin Hardcastle emerged from his saloon. He nodded to Cruz, then spoke to Riley. "When you get through with that, come in and have a drink."

It was warm and pleasant in the street. Riley ignored Shattuck until the cattleman rode on down, to draw up before the Bon-Ton Saloon, where he dismounted. He stood there on the walk, talking with Doc Beaman, and then they went into the Bon-Ton together.

When he had finished the packing, Riley indicated the saloon. "Let's go in and see what he has to offer."

Cruz did not like Hardcastle, so he shook his head. "There is a cantina," he said, "and a girl to whom I must say goodbye. If the señor will permit—?"

"Of course."

Hardcastle placed a bottle on the bar when Riley came in. "Help yourself," he said. "This is on me. Glad to welcome a newcomer into the country."

Spooner was nowhere about, but another man, a square, untidy man, lounged alone at a rear table. Nick Valentz stared at Riley, then looked away. Now where had he seen *him* before?

Hardcastle poured drinks. "Shattuck's a difficult man," he said. "Big-headed, too."

Riley lifted his glass. "Here's how!" he said, and downed the drink. Hardcastle had something on his mind, and Riley intended to learn what it was.

"I know where you can get some white-face cattle," Hardcastle said. "Not many, but enough to start a herd."

Riley was surprised. "Herefords?"

"Yes. You'd have to drive them down from Moab—there's only about thirty head."

"Bull among them?"

"Yes."

"How much?"

Martin Hardcastle took a cigar from his vest pocket and clipped the end with strong white teeth, then studied the cigar for a moment while he framed his answer. He put the cigar between his teeth and struck a match. Looking past the cigar as he lifted the match, he said, "Five dollars a head if you run them on the mesa between Indian and Cottonwood creeks."

Gaylord Riley always liked to know what was going on in a community, so he said, "Whose range is that?"

"Open range."

The offer smelled of trouble—all kinds of trouble. The price was far too cheap.

"Too far from my place," he said. "How much otherwise?"

"That's a good offer, and it's a good range."

"The offer is too good. Whose toes do you want stepped on?"

Hardcastle hesitated. This man was no fool, but how far would he go to get some white-face cattle? He decided against showing his hand. "Forget it. You can have the cattle for twenty dollars a head. I had an idea I'd show Shattuck a thing or two. He figures he's the only man around here who can have any Herefords."

"My range is farther out," Riley said mildly. "But at twenty per head, I'll buy."

Hardcastle shrugged. "Okay . . . it was a fool idea, anyway." He put his cigar down and picked up a pen. "Darby Lewis works for you, and he knows where these cattle are. You send him for them. No need to go yourself unless you're of a mind to."

That suited Riley, for he wished to get back to the ranch at the head of Fable Canyon as soon as possible.

"You send Darby, and I'll have a hand of mine ride with him to your range."

"All right." Riley placed his glass on the bar. He looked right into Hardcastle's eyes. "Just one thing, Mr. Hardcastle. I don't know you, and you don't know me. Across the street Mr. Burrage will tell you I'm good for the money, but when those cattle arrive, I want a bill of sale, and I want clear brands, d'you hear?"

Martin Hardcastle did not like to be questioned. Irritation stirred within him, but he stifled it. "Of course. This is a legitimate deal."

"And no cattle that ever—at any time—belonged to Shattuck."

"Shattuck never saw these cattle."

"Fine—fine and dandy. You've made yourself a deal."

As he walked through the door, Hardcastle stared after him. *So have you,* he said in his mind. *So have you, you young fool.*

*   *   *

From the moment of Gaylord Riley's arrival in town and his expression of interest in white-face cattle, Hardcastle had seen in him a tool for the destruction of Dan Shattuck.

Martin Hardcastle was, up to a point, a reasonable man. Like many a man who has enjoyed consistent success, he had come to believe anything he decided on was right, and to be infuriated by anyone or anything that tried to stand in his way. And Martin Hardcastle's success had never suffered frustration until that day when he approached Dan Shattuck.

It was not so much the refusal, but Shattuck's shocked astonishment at his suggestion, that angered Hardcastle. He had believed his association with the women in the house by the river was unknown, and over the months of his staring at Marie he had convinced himself there was nothing impossible in his plan. After all, he was a rich man—quite as rich as Shattuck, when it came to that, and between the two of them they could control everything around.

As he watched Marie coming and going about the town, he fancied she was not unaware of him, and when he combed his hair before the mirror he told himself he was a handsome man—so why not Marie? And after all, who else was there?

From the days when he had been a shoulder-striker in the streets of New York for Tom Poole, Martin Hardcastle had climbed the ladder of success steadily. It did not matter to him that several of the rungs had been the bodies of men who got in the way, or that his two hard fists and a hard skull had helped his success quite as much as what was inside his skull.

From a repeat voter and hired slugger, he had gone on to become a watchman at a gambling house, a gambler, master of a bawdy house, and finally, owner of his own gambling joint.

Aware that any further success would interfere with more powerful interests in New York, he was preparing to leave when the unfortunate death of a man he had rolled made leaving imperative. He had gone to Pittsburgh, to St. Louis, to

New Orleans, and then he had followed the railroads west, operating a "house" at the end-of-the-line towns.

The sudden birth of Rimrock had offered opportunity and he had moved in, opened his own saloon, and then bought another. He had prospered immediately, the saloons crowded, the house on the river doing a land-office business. He bought the livery stable, and opened a store close by. He had been doing a little business buying and selling stock, and kept a corral behind the livery stable where there were weekly auctions of stock. He also operated a butcher shop that sold meat locally.

He had left the ranch of Dan Shattuck that day trembling with cold fury, a fury that turned into hatred. Never for an instant had his resolve weakened. He intended to have Marie.

Of course, she was unaware of his meeting with Shattuck, and he was sure Shattuck would not speak of it. Regardless of that, he intended at the first opportunity to speak to her himself.

But he was no fool. He was quite sure that Dan Shattuck had meant what he said when he threatened to have him horsewhipped if he tried to speak to Marie.

He had made up his mind. He would have Marie, but before he had her he would destroy Dan Shattuck, and nowhere would he show his hand. The instrument for Shattuck's destruction would be this young rancher and his white-face cattle.

When Riley had gone, Valentz came from his table to the bar. "I've seen that gent some place before this—can't figure where."

"When you remember," Hardcastle said, "you come to me—and don't you tell anybody but me."

Valentz was surprised, for he had not gathered that Riley was important. He accepted a drink, and leaned on the bar, trying to think back. From the instant he had glimpsed Riley he had known his face. He had changed, no doubt; a fellow that young might change a lot in a few years. Maybe if he started thinking of him as younger . . . maybe that would do it.

But even as Hardcastle made his plans to have Marie, other plans were being made. They were being shaped right outside his own door. And the man doing the shaping was Strat Spooner.

FIVE

Gaylord Riley, followed by Cruz and three pack horses, arrived at the ranch site late in the afternoon.

The ride had been long and hard, but for the last few miles he had hurried the pace, eager to be on the ground and in camp before darkness. Moreover, he wanted time to look around, to see if anyone had been there during his absence.

He no longer—in fact, he had never—thought of himself as an outlaw, yet his friends were outlaws and they were in dire trouble, and now, if ever, they would need him.

Nothing at the ranch site had changed. He rode out on the bench with Cruz and looked around; the usual deer tracks were there, and among them, over some of them, the tracks of a stalking lion.

As they drew up, the low wall of the aspen and pine-clad Sweet Alice Hills was behind them, cutting them off from the view to the east. Westward the land was afire . . . the pinks and reds of the fantastic rock formations to the west and north were weirdly lit by the dull red fire of the setting sun, while the dark fingers of canyon that clawed toward the Colorado were simply black streaks through the crimson.

Cruz looked at the scene with astonishment, then crossed himself. "It is a devil's land," he whispered. "I had heard of it, but—not—never like this!"

"We're eight thousand feet up," Riley said quietly, "and it is here I have begun to build, here I shall live.

"Right down there in front of us is Fable Canyon, and we'll hold our stock there through the worst of the winter. The rest of the time we'll graze them on the plateaus or over in the basin to the north. There's thousands of acres of good grazing over there, but we can't run too many head. This country won't stand overgrazing. I've seen it done, and seen thistles come in, and sage . . . the cattle won't eat them."

He pointed to their left front. "That's Dark Canyon Plateau— stretches away for miles. On our right front is Wild Cow Point. To the north, with those canyons feeding into it, is the basin. There are springs over there, but we'll put a couple of small dams in to hold back some of the run-off.

"If we hold the numbers down, with white-face cattle we can make out. They will build on more beef to the head than longhorns. Taking them all around, the Hereford or white-face is the best animal for this country. They make out better where they have to rustle for grub, and they stand the weather."

Jim Colburn knew of this place, and could find his way here if he was in any condition to do so, and he would use his head about making himself known.

Riley was thinking now about Cruz. He found himself liking the lean, whiplike Mexican. The man missed very little, and he was a good worker. He was altogether a different kind of a man from Darby Lewis, who had ridden to Moab for the cattle.

Lewis was a casual, lackadaisical sort, an efficient cowhand, but the sort who would one day draw his time and ride into town, simply because he had enough money saved, or was tired of working. Also—and it was a quality Riley did not welcome—he was inclined to be talkative. With the visitors he must expect, such a quality was not desirable.

They stripped the gear from their horses and made camp. Again and again Cruz looked at the country about them. "It is beautiful, *amigo*," he said at last. "I do not wonder that you like it here."

They camped in the open, under the trees. The walls of the house had been started, and Riley had built a pole corral. Their camp was only a few yards from the corral where they left their horses, but from the camp they had a good view of the country around and of the trail over which they had come.

Sheriff Ed Larsen might be as innocent as he seemed, and he might also be willing to let bygones be bygones if he did guess that Gaylord Riley was one of the old Colburn gang; but Riley was not buying it.

At daylight he rolled out of his warm bed, and in the chill air he hustled a fire together and got the coffeepot on. The morning air was incredibly clear, and as he worked he listened, for sound would carry far.

Cruz rolled out, dressed, and went to the corral to catch up their horses, saddling them both without comment and returning to the fire. While breakfast shaped up, Riley scanned the country. Twice he saw movement in the distance; at least once it was a deer. As to the other movement, he was not sure. The glimpse was too momentary to offer anything but a suspicion, but he believed it to be a man—and there should be no other men anywhere around.

While Cruz straightened up around camp, Riley walked a wide circle around, checking the ground. He saw no tracks but those he had seen the night before, but he did find a dim and ancient trail that apparently led to the top of the Sweet Alice Hills, about five hundred feet above the ranch. He would remember that, and try it. From up there a man could see just about all over the country.

All the long day through, they rode, down Fable Canyon and by a dim trail over the shoulder of Wild Cow Point and into the basin. They scouted the two springs, located a seep in another place, and chose a couple of spots for small dams.

Moving away from the southernmost of the springs, Riley suddenly saw the tracks near the mouth of a canyon. At least six horses, all shod, traveling in a bunch. He did not wish to draw attention to the trail, so he scarcely glanced at it.

He was riding some dozen feet away from Cruz at the time, and the tracks were off to his right and out of the range of the Mexican's eyes, so Riley veered over toward him and they rode up the canyon, across the shoulder of the mountain, and back to their own ranch. By the time they arrived it was dark.

Six horses . . . four men and two pack animals? Or six men of a posse? The tracks were fresh—very likely made that morning, around sunup. Possibly even later. Cruz was no fool, and if he saw those tracks he would be curious.

"We'll work on the house tomorrow," Riley said, "if you've no objection to working off a horse." Many cowhands would do no work that could not be done from a saddle, and were offended by the suggestion. "There's plenty to do right here."

Worried as he was about Colburn and the others, Riley became fascinated by the task before him. He was building a house . . . a home. Never in his life had he had what might properly be called a home, and most of his years had been lived out under the sky. But these very logs he was laying in place, these were the walls of the house where, with luck, he would live out his years.

Obsessed by the thought, he drove himself, working harder and faster, until Cruz finally straightened up and drew back. "There is always tomorrow, *amigo*," he said gently.

Riley straightened up, a little embarrassed. "Of course." He looked across the building at Cruz. "It is just that I never had a home before."

"Ah?"

Cruz lit a cigarette. "All the more reason then, to build carefully, build to last."

He indicated the blisters on Riley's hands. "I think it is a long time since you have worked with your hands, *amigo*."

He said no more than that, and Riley offered no comment, nor any explanation. Cruz missed very little, and the longer Riley worked with him the better he liked him.

On the third day Riley rode out again with Cruz, and killed a deer. It was a good shot, a running shot, and he broke the deer's neck just above the shoulder.

That night, they talked long beside the fire, and Riley added a little to what he had learned from the file of newspapers in the office of the *Rimrock Scout*. The picture he was getting was filled in a little here and there, and from the picture three men were beginning to emerge.

Dan Shattuck . . . Martin Hardcastle . . . and Sheriff Ed Larsen.

He sorted them over in his mind, put a label to each, and dealt the cards again, studying them with care. For he was a stranger in a strange land; he was a man with much behind him, and a lifetime yet to live, and those three might all take a hand in his game. It would be well to know them, to understand them thoroughly.

That was something, too, he had learned from Jim Colburn, for Jim's success was due not only to careful planning of the robberies and the escapes, but to his study of the men employed in the various banks, or the drivers on the stages.

Which would be apt to take a chance? Was this one trying to build a reputation? Was that one nervous? Was he angry with his wife and apt to take it out on anyone? Was that one cautious? This one reckless? Which ones had families to think of?

So now Riley studied the men in the case. Shattuck with his vast acres, his white-face cattle, and Marie, his niece. Of these things he was proud; of his family background too, and of his honor and integrity.

Martin Hardcastle? A pusher and a climber, a man of vast ego, vastly sure of himself, a man with a lust for power, for name.

Sheriff Ed Larsen? An old man, a careful man, a man unafraid. He was a Mormon, and in good-standing with the Church. He had come west with the Handcart Mormons as a child—the Mormons, most of them from Europe, who walked across the plains pushing their few belongings in handcarts.

And in Rimrock, loitering around Hardcastle's saloon, and

occasionally riding out of town on what missions nobody knew, was Strat Spooner. And Spooner harbored his own lusts and his own desires.

A raw-boned man who thrust his big bare feet into his boots without the benefit of socks, whose shirt collars were greasy and long-unwashed, Strat Spooner was Martin Hardcastle's man only up to a point. The West held many riders who rode for the brand, men who were feudal retainers in all that term might imply, possessed of fierce loyalty to the outfit, the brand, and the boss. Strat Spooner was not one of these. He was a mercenary, a man with a gun for hire, occasional rustler, thief, and killer, a dangerous gunman whose only loyalty was to himself. He served, but he served for money. His loyalty always appeared obvious, but it was always given with reservations.

Strat Spooner had often been contemptuous of those for whom he worked, but he was not contemptuous of Martin Hardcastle. He knew the saloonkeeper was a dangerous man, but he had no idea that Hardcastle was interested in Marie Shattuck. Had he known, it would have made no difference.

Strat Spooner wanted Marie Shattuck with a savage lust that he was shrewd enough to realize could get him killed. He knew enough about the temper of western towns to know that a hanging would be the least he could get from molesting a woman—if he was caught.

Nor did he like the look of old Pico. The Mexican was a hard, capable man, an excellent tracker, a bad man with a gun, and a man who seemed to have a sixth sense of guessing what another man might do.

Marie Shattuck was not merely a pretty girl, not merely a bright one with character; she was a girl born with that particular something that brought excitement to every man who looked at her.

Even as Hardcastle was making his plans, Strat Spooner sat on the walk outside thinking of his own. He had no such concrete plans as Hardcastle had, for he was not that sort of man. He would wait, and he would watch, and when the opportunity came he would take it . . . and her.

Thirty-two head of white-face cattle arrived at Rimrock on the drive from Moab. Darby Lewis and two hands working for Hardcastle drove them, rounding them up to bed down on a small meadow just outside of town. Standing in the door of his saloon, Hardcastle saw Lewis and one of the other hands ride into town.

They had made good time—better than he had expected; and now that they were here the first part of his plan could go forward. Before he was through Dan Shattuck would be broke and broken, and Marie would be glad to have any man who would take her.

There was nothing in the mind of Martin Hardcastle that allowed for half measures. When he set out to destroy an enemy, it was with the idea of doing so utterly and completely, for he wished nothing left behind that might rise to take revenge on him.

He was going to destroy Dan Shattuck and have Marie, and Gaylord Riley was going to be the instrument of their destruction. The small herd of white-face cattle was the opening wedge. The further steps in his plan were awaiting execution.

The words came to him, and he liked their sound. He repeated them to himself: *awaiting execution.*

SIX

When Riley worked at the walls of the house he was building he could look out over the country around him, and it was an empty land. Yet it had not always been so.

There were cliff dwellings in Fable Canyon, there were other ruins in several of the neighboring canyons and in the basin. Who were those people? Where had they come from, and where had they gone? Above all, why had they gone?

Since the Navajo had been moved from Bosque Redondo and settled in northern New Mexico, a few had drifted into the vast lands south of the Colorado and San Juan rivers, but none had come up into this country. Occasionally, Ute war parties had ridden through, but they had been few and far between.

It was a haunted, mysterious land, and the ghosts of those all but forgotten people lingered. The thought of them was often at the fringes of Riley's mind.

During the weeks that followed his arrival in the Sweet Alice Hills he had prowled about several of the ruins. An olla which hung under a large tree, keeping water cold for them, had been found in one of those ruins and carefully cleaned. There were fragments of pottery, arrowheads, a few scrapers—these things he recognized. The problem of the vanished people intrigued him, but there was little time for his mind to dwell long on such things.

Among the white-face cattle that had been driven down from Moab were a few good ones, but most of them were no better than average. The bull was old, but showed evidences of good breeding. They kept the cattle close herded on the mesa close by, letting them get acquainted with their new home and the route to a seep in nearby Dark Canyon.

During the first week they killed two mountain lions, one of them while it was engrossed in feeding on a young deer. It was more than a week after the discovery of the tracks of the six horses in the basin before Riley managed to go back to the place alone. Here and there the passage of deer or flurries of dust had almost wiped them out, but Riley worked out the trail.

They had followed a wash out of the basin and had gone along the mesa's top, over a saddle and into a deep pocket in the hills that lay under the east rim of Horse Mountain. Here a camp had been made, but now the camp was deserted.

Restless and worried, Riley prowled about, studying the sign. On the edge of the fire he found a tiny fragment of blood-stained cloth, charred along the edges, evidently a bandage. He found the footprints of three men, and a place where grass and pine needles had been heaped up to make a cushion beneath a bedroll. Around this there were a number of boot tracks.

Three men on their feet, then, and one down. Riley walked about, checking every aspect of the camp.

There was no water. The nearest spring was about two miles south, and they had carried water to this place—evidence that they feared pursuit and wanted to be away from any known water hole. Following a dim trail to the crest of Horse Mountain, over a thousand feet above the Pocket, he discovered where a man had waited, keeping watch. From that point on the mountain all the trails could be watched.

Returning to the deserted camp, he looked around a while longer. There was enough evidence to convince him that it had indeed been the camp of Jim Colburn and the others. He knew all the little tricks and devices they used for making a camp easier, knew them too well to be mistaken.

On the mountain, Kehoe and Colburn had taken turns watching the trails. He knew this from the cigar and cigarette butts he found there. And he was quite sure it had been Weaver who was hurt. They had remained in camp for at least a week, and four men had ridden away, with two pack horses.

Reassured, Riley left the camp and turned his horse and followed the mesa toward the southwest, picking up an ancient Indian trail, barely discernible at this hour—for night was coming on. He followed it across the head of Trail Canyon to Dark Canyon Plateau, and had just started to climb out of the hollow that headed Trail Canyon when he heard, some distance off, a stone rattle against rocks.

He drew up, listening.

The coming of darkness had brought coolness; not a breath of air seemed to be stirring. He listened for several minutes, and heard nothing more, yet he was positive there had been something down in that canyon . . . something not an animal, but a man. He could not have explained why he was sure that what he had heard was a man, but his every instinct warned him that it was so.

When he rode back to the ranch site there was a good fire going. Cruz was sitting near it, tending the supper. Darby Lewis was working at a riata he was braiding from thin strips of cowhide.

Cruz glanced up at Riley, but offered no comment. It was Darby who spoke. "Ridin' late," he said. "I was hopin' you'd shoot us a deer."

"Only saw one—too far off."

Riley dismounted and stripped the gear from his horse. He would have to ride into Rimrock, he was thinking. They needed more horses, and he wanted to look around for cattle.

*   *   *

Marie Shattuck was curious. She had met Gaylord Riley for
only a moment, but he kept coming back to her mind . . . and
he was good-looking.

Peg Oliver met her as she was leaving her buckboard. "Marie,
didn't you tell me you'd met Gaylord Riley? That new rancher?"

"Yes, I met him."

"We're having a party at the ranch. Why don't you invite
him?"

"I don't know him that well." She hesitated. "Anyway, I
don't think Uncle Dan would like it."

"You're the only one who has met him, and all the girls have
been hoping he would come over. He hasn't been to a party
yet."

"He's pretty busy, I expect. Anyway, it is a long way from
his place to yours."

"Marie, you know darned well that never stopped anybody! Why, some of the boys ride thirty or forty miles for
a dance."

"Well . . . if I see him."

Sheriff Ed Larsen sat in the Bon-Ton with Sampson McCarty,
and the newspaperman knew that, no matter how placid Larsen
might look to others, he was worried.

"Peaceful community," Larsen mumbled, at McCarty's
question. "I want to keep it that way."

McCarty glanced at him sharply. "Is something in the wind?"

"Too much riding arount at night," Larsen said grumpily.
"And no sign of the Colburn outfit. Dey dropped clean off the
edge of the worlt."

Just then Darby Lewis opened the door and walked in,
waving a hand. McCarty gestured to the chair opposite. "Sit
down . . . buy you a cup of coffee."

Darby grinned. "I'll do that—although I will say that Mex
makes good coffee."

"Cruz? He's a good man." McCarty paused. "How d' you like your new job?"

"Ain't bad—but he ain't got enough cows to make it a good ridin' job. Too much damn hand work. Buildin' the house, fences, and the like."

"Fences?"

"Uh-huh—he's fencin' off some of the plateaus. That way he can keep track of his stock until they get to know where home is."

Darby Lewis sipped the coffee appreciatively. "That Riley knows cattle," he said.

He went on to tell them about the house, the corrals, the dams. Larsen listened, but asked no questions. It was obvious that this Riley was a man who had come to stay. He was doing work that would have long-range effect.

"Has he said anything about mining?" Larsen asked, trying to find out more about him.

"Not much. He's done some placer minin'—he mentioned that, one time."

McCarty's back was to the door, but Larsen was watching when the two strange riders drew up before Hardcastle's saloon. They were dusty, and their horses were weary. When the two riders stepped down from the saddle they stood for a moment, straightening their backs, as men are apt to do who have ridden far.

The men were strangers to Rimrock and one of them wore two guns. Their brands were strange, and both rode double-cinched saddles of the Texas kind.

Gunmen . . . ?

"Ain't seen Spooner around for a few days," McCarty commented suddenly.

"He's here now," Darby said. "He rode in just after we did."

Gaylord Riley walked slowly along the short street of Rimrock. He had seen Strat Spooner ride into town, and he had seen him take his horse to the livery stable. And that horse had seen some riding.

Was it coincidence that Spooner had arrived so soon after Riley and Darby Lewis had reached town? Or had Spooner been following him?

His two years on the outlaw trail and his years before that of hunting down the men who killed his father had made him wary. He watched his back trail always, and he was suspicious of sounds, of motives, of movements.

So far as he knew he was not a wanted man, but Colburn and the others were, and Spooner might be a bounty hunter. Undoubtedly there were reward offers on all four of them.

Hardcastle was the town's stock dealer and it was to him that Riley went to buy horses. Stepping through the bat-wing doors into the saloon, he noticed two men deep in conversation with Spooner and Hardcastle at the far end of the bar. When he came in, Hardcastle looked up, then walked up the bar toward him.

"How are you, Riley? What'll you have?"

The two men glanced his way. Spooner said something to them in a low tone, and they looked once more. One of the men shook his head.

"I'll have rye whiskey, and then we'll talk horses—if you have any to sell."

Hardcastle took a bottle from beneath the bar and filled two glasses. "You'd do better to buy them yourself," he said affably. "It would save you money. I haven't anything you'd be likely to want, but I hear Oliver out at the Boxed O has a few head."

He lifted his glass. "Luck," he said, and then commented, "Too bad Shattuck wouldn't sell you some of his Herefords. You're going to need more cattle."

"I'm in the market."

"About those horses," Hardcastle said. "Oliver might not want to sell. I hear that Shattuck has put the word out."

"What do you mean . . . 'the word'?"

"Not to sell to you. He wants to be the only man around with any Herefords. He's afraid if anybody else has them there'll be some rustling of his stock."

"He needn't worry."

Riley finished his drink and went outside, pausing on the street. The words of Hardcastle had made almost no impression, in part because Riley rarely took for granted what he was told about other people, finding most gossip malicious or irresponsible, and based on the most fragile of rumors. What he was thinking about was the two men at the end of the bar; he had seen neither of them before, but he knew their type.

Their horses, tied at the hitch-rail, supplied what he had only guessed. They were from Texas—he recognized one of the brands; and the double cinch was still almost a Texas monopoly—and they were gunhands for hire. The horses they rode were too good, their saddles and other gear were too expensive for ordinary cowhands.

But why here . . . in Rimrock? Such men followed the tides of cattle wars, and feuds, and there was nothing of the kind in northern Arizona or southern Utah.

Bounty hunters? They could be.

Absently, he noticed the Boxed O on a buckboard in front of the general store, and turned that way.

Peg Oliver was little, plump, and attractive, one of those merry, friendly, outgoing girls, liked by everyone. She was talking to Darby Lewis when he saw them.

Darby turned to greet him. "Boss, this here's Peg Oliver. They're throwing a wind-ding out at their place, an' we're invited."

She turned to Riley, her eyes bright and eager. "Will you come, Mr. Riley? After all, you'll want to get acquainted with your neighbors, and they'll all be there."

He hesitated, then nodded. "Yes, we'll come, and thank you." He started to speak about the horses, then decided against it. That could wait until he met her father.

Sampson McCarty came to the door of his office and motioned to Riley.

"Will you excuse me, Miss Oliver? I'll see you at the dance."

McCarty's eyes twinkled. "See you've been roped—be careful she doesn't hog-tie you."

Riley grinned. "No danger. I'm right skittish around womenfolks. Never had much experience thataway."

"Then you're in more trouble than I thought. If you're going to escape women, you have to know something about them—and even that doesn't help."

"You wanted to see me?"

"Uh-huh. You were looking for white-face or Shorthorn cattle. I've got a tip for you." He went inside and Riley followed him.

"I like to see a young man try to better himself, and I just heard about this. You've been asking about Herefords and Durhams—or Shorthorns, if you want to call them so. Well, do you know where Spanish Fork is?"

"Yes."

"A tenderfoot named Beaman heard about the Texas trail drives, and he decided to make one from Oregon. He bought up three thousand head of mixed Durhams and Herefords, with a few odds and ends of dairy cattle among them, and started east for Kansas.

"His trail drivers quit him in Spanish Fork. They heard about the Sioux outbreak in Wyoming and Nebraska, and they wanted no part of it. He's holding those cattle outside of Spanish Fork—at least he was last week. And he's ready to sell."

Riley thought of the country between Rimrock and Spanish Fork, much of which he knew. The Outlaw Trail led through that country—a trail known to none but outlaws and Indians; and a wild, wild country it was. Bringing cattle down the main trail would be sheer insanity, for there were farms, hayfields—such a herd could do more damage than they were worth. But if a man knew the water holes . . .

"Hadn't you heard?" he said. "Shattuck doesn't want anybody to sell to me—or so they tell me."

McCarty shrugged. "Shattuck's a good man, but he's a dog-in-the-manger about those Herefords of his. Anyway, he had his chance and turned it down."

Riley stared at him, waiting.

"He turned it down because he said the man didn't live who could bring those cattle down here without paying damages to every farmer between here and there."

"So why tell me?"

McCarty smiled faintly. "I thought you might have some other ideas."

SEVEN

The Boxed O ranch house was wide and sprawling. Oliver was a Gentile from Illinois, and one who had been friendly to the Mormons through their difficulties there and in Missouri; as a result had been disliked by some of his neighbors. Migrating west, he had settled among the Mormons, and his ranch had for fifteen years been a headquarters for the settlers in the vicinity and a hotel for travelers through the country.

At first these had been very few, then the flow of travel increased, but settlers were few and far between in the vast, wide-open country where he had chosen to live. Dan Shattuck had been his first actual neighbor, and their ranches were miles apart.

From the first, Oliver's ranch had been different from others in the Southwest, for, like his Mormon friends, he did not rely strictly on beef cattle. He had planted corn, wheat, and rye, and he had grown vegetables, raised chickens, and kept bees. From the beginning, the operation had been successful, self-supporting after the first year, and a money-making venture in most of the years that followed.

Gaylord Riley stopped in a cottonwood grove a few miles

from the ranch and peeled off his range clothes. He took a dip in the stream, then dressed in the black broadcloth suit he had bought on his last trip to California. He packed his range clothes in his slicker and rolled them behind his saddle, remounted, and rode on to the Oliver ranch.

Half a dozen buckboards already stood in the ranch yard, and the hitch-rail and corral fences were lined with the mounts of the cowhands and others who had ridden in from around the country.

He hesitated in the darkness after tying his horse. He brushed his clothes with his hand, tried the crease in his sombrero, and ran a finger around inside his shirt collar. It was a long time since he had worn a collar and tie.

The last time had been in Los Angeles when the Colburn gang had ridden into town for a celebration. Unknown there, they had passed themselves off as ranchers and horse buyers from Arizona, and had taken rooms at the fashionable Pico House. They had come to town to relax, smoke good cigars, eat meals they did not have to cook, and drink the best of wine.

Now, standing there in the darkness, looking at the laughing, talking groups on the wide verandas, Riley was glad he had had those few weeks on the coast. It had given him one of the few chances in his life to meet people other than cowhands or outlaws.

There had been little enough to do but attend the new Merced Theatre next door to the hotel or stand on the walk outside and watch the stages come in from Wilmington, but it had given him the chance to meet people. Surprisingly, it was Kehoe who taught him what he needed to know, for the tall Irish outlaw had the manners of a gentleman when in company, and carried himself with a certain elegance that Riley had done his best to imitate.

It was Kehoe with his easy, friendly ways and polished manner who made friends, and they were invited, Kehoe and himself, to some of the best homes in town.

Nevertheless, he had never gotten over a certain shyness when among strangers, and now he walked slowly toward the house, realizing he would know no more than one or two of the people here.

Everyone was welcome, he understood that, but he was wary of encountering someone who might know him from elsewhere. It was this as much as his natural shyness that held him back.

Finally, after one reassuring touch on his gun to make sure he had it, he approached the house. People glanced at him, and several turned to look after he passed. Self-consciously, he went up the steps.

The first person he glimpsed as he stepped through the door was Marie Shattuck. She had turned toward the door as he stepped in, and for an instant she remained still, staring at him, startled at his unexpected arrival.

"Miss Shattuck?" He spoke in his best Kehoe style. "It is good to see you again."

"Why, yes—I didn't know . . . I mean I wasn't expecting to see you here."

"I invited him." Peg Oliver was suddenly beside her. "After all, we can't let him think we aren't hospitable."

Across the room he saw Dan Shattuck turn and glance toward him, and saw the older man's expression change and become bleak.

"I can't stay long," he said. "I've got a long ride before me."

"You're leaving?" Marie was surprised at the intensity of her own voice, and saw Peg glance at her suddenly.

"To buy cattle," he said. "I heard of some I can buy—if I hurry."

Dan Shattuck was suddenly beside them. "If you mean the herd at Spanish Fork," he said, "you'd be wasting your time. The farmers along the trail will not allow any trail herds to come through."

"I'll bring them through."

Dan Shattuck was irritated. This young man disturbed him and aroused his ire, and that very fact served to nettle him even more. Why should he worry what Riley did? Only . . . his were the only white-face herd in the Territory, and he was proud of the fact. Also, there was that matter of rustling—as long as his were the only cattle of the kind, his herd was relatively safe. But which was the more important reason?

"You'll have to have hands," he said, "and they aren't easy to find. But even with enough cowhands, there's no way you could get those cattle through without sprouting wings on them."

The music had started and Riley turned quickly to Marie. "Will you dance with me?" He spoke quickly, before her uncle could interrupt, and in an instant, while Dan Shattuck's face hardened with anger, they were out on the floor with the others.

"He's a handsome man, Uncle Dan," Peg said, "and he likes Marie."

"He's a damned fool!" Shattuck replied roughly, and strode away.

Gaylord Riley danced well, for he was a man handy with his feet, and with rhythm in his blood, and there had been times here and there about the country when he had danced with girls from the Rio Grande to the Sacramento.

"You dance well, Mr. Riley," Marie said.

"It is because I dance with you," he said, and was surprised at how easily the words came to him.

"Are you going to stay with us, then?"

"Yes."

"You must not let Uncle Dan worry you. He is a good man, but very proud."

"There are too many other things about which to worry," he said, then looking down at her: "I have not known many girls."

"I don't believe that," she said quickly, and added, "Peg likes you."

"I like her," he agreed, "and she thought to ask me over."

Suddenly the small talk died within him. A thin, stooped man, his face deep-lined, was standing at the far side of the room. He wore a low-slung gun, and his eyes were watching Riley.

"What's the matter?" Marie asked quickly. "You sure you're feeling well?"

"I never felt better," he said, "but let's get off the floor."

That man was Desloge, an outlaw, one Riley had met and known slightly near Lordsburg—at a town called Shakespeare, actually. What was he doing *here*, of all places?

He had never liked the man, and Jim had refused Desloge sharply when he suggested he throw in with the Colburn gang. He was a hired gunman, but the stories about him went beyond that. Several times he had outlaw companions who disappeared abruptly, and others who found themselves in the hands of the law under peculiar circumstances. Nobody could prove a thing, but too much had happened to be mere coincidence.

And now he was here, and Riley was sure the man had recognized him.

How long had it been? Most of two years, and Riley had changed—but not enough.

They stood together on the porch, with other couples around them, and they talked quietly. For the first time Riley forgot who he was and what he had been, and was simply a man talking to a girl. From time to time he was aware that a number of young men wanted to interrupt, but all of them hesitated.

Desloge appeared in the door, and Riley saw his eyes darting this way and that, searching. It was time to ride out.

Suddenly he saw Darby Lewis out at the edge of the light. "Marie," he said quickly, "there's Darby Lewis. I've been watching for him, and it's time to go. Will you excuse me?"

Before she could even reply he threw a leg over the porch rail and dropped to the ground. A moment later he disappeared into the night with Darby. Nettled, she stared after him in the darkness.

Peg Oliver came up beside her. "What happened, Marie? What did you say to him?"

"Nothing. We were just talking, and all of a sudden he excused himself and disappeared."

She was irritated, and somewhat taken aback by the sudden leave-taking. Had she offended him somehow? But how?

Surprisingly, she was dismayed and hurt. It was not like her to be worried by what any man might do, and there was no reason for her feeling so now. Certainly, he had said nothing to her to lead her to believe he was interested in her. And she was definitely not interested in him.

Definitely . . .

She was still telling herself that hours later, when she lay in bed. And then for the first time she remembered something else.

That strange man standing in the doorway—the one with the lined face. In the moment before they left the dance floor she had seen him—was he the reason for Gaylord Riley's sudden wish to go out on the porch? And later to disappear into the darkness?

She was imagining things. . . . Only, that man had been there both times, and he had seemed to be looking for someone.

She must remember, and tomorrow she must find out who he was.

She snuggled deeper under the blankets, for the night was chill. She went to sleep remembering how Gaylord Riley moved and talked, and the way he looked at her. There was something strange about him, strange and exciting.

Cruz was awake when they rode in, leading the four extra saddle horses Oliver had sold them. The Mexican got up and strolled over.

"Get some sleep," Riley suggested. "Tomorrow we ride to Spanish Fork."

When Darby had led the horses away, Cruz said, "Somebody should stay here. I have seen tracks."

"Fresh tracks?"

"Sí."

"Many riders? Or one?"

"One only . . . he watches."

Riley was relieved. One rider would scarcely mean the Colburn outfit. Yet who could it be? Was it the man who had been in Trail Canyon that night when Riley returned from checking the outlaw camp? If, indeed, there had even been a man.

Despite the need for sleep before the long ride, he lay awake for some time, pondering the situation. Why was Desloge in Rimrock? And who were the two strange riders talking to Spooner? Three gunhands in the space of a couple of days could not be coincidence. Trouble was breeding, but for whom?

He lay staring up at the stars, hearing the remote sounds as night and the cooling of the rocks brought little movements to the darkness.

What must Marie think of him? He had left her so abruptly. . . .

One thing he knew. He did not wish to talk to Desloge, nor to be seen talking to him. He had left all that behind him—or had he?

EIGHT

Darby Lewis was a good sleeper, and the light rain that commenced to fall shortly before daybreak lulled him into an even deeper sleep. He did not hear the soft hoof-falls of the horse, nor did he hear the hooting of a lonely owl.

Cruz did hear the owl. It was the wrong time for an owl to be hooting, and Cruz was a man alive to such things. He awakened, but lay still, listening.

Gaylord Riley rose swiftly and silently, belted on his gun, and picked up his hat and slicker. The three men were bedded down on the floor of the newly completed room, but Riley had been closest to the door. He opened it without a sound, and stepped out into the night.

Cruz lay still and listened. He heard Riley's footsteps as he walked through the rain, heard him pause, and then the splash of heavier steps, and a low voice.

Rising silently, with a glance at the sleeping form of Darby Lewis, Cruz stepped to the window, closed only by shutters. Through a crack he could see the dim outlines of a man on horseback and of Riley; and then the two walked away toward the lean-to that had been doing duty as kitchen and dining hall.

Riley stirred up the coals and added fuel, moving the coffee-pot to the hottest of the coals. Cruz watched for a few moments, but he was unable to see the stranger's face. It was chilly, and anyway this was Riley's own business. After a little while he returned to his bed and went to sleep.

The man under the lean-to with Riley was Kehoe. "You've got things going here, kid," he said. "I think you'll have yourself a place."

"Part of it is yours."

"Maybe. We'll see."

He accepted the coffee gratefully, and Riley studied his face. The Irishman looked drawn and tired.

"We've had a run of bad luck," Kehoe said. "Weaver caught one, but he's all right now."

"I found your camp over back of Horse Mountain."

Kehoe chuckled. "I told Parrish you'd find it. He didn't think so."

He sipped his coffee, warming his fingers around the cup. Suddenly he looked up. "You had any trouble?"

"No."

"You will have. The word's around that somebody up this way is in the market for gunmen. You remember Desloge?"

"I've seen him. He's here."

"He's doin' the hiring, and he's teamed up with a Wyoming pistol-fighter named Enloe, Gus Enloe. They're mean—poison mean."

Kehoe huddled nearer the fire. His coat was thin and wet. "You want my slicker?" Riley asked.

"No . . . lost mine a while back." Kehoe refilled the cup. "Tell me about this set-up."

Riley, sitting on a log, told him quietly and as concisely as possible about Shattuck, about the cattle he had bought, and Shattuck's resentment of him. He also mentioned the impending ride to Spanish Fork. The sky was growing gray before Kehoe stood up.

"Got to be goin', Lord." The nickname brought back old

times. Kehoe put down his cup. "You're doing all right. Now stay with it."

"I need hands for the drive from the Fork."

Kehoe glanced at him. "Hell, I wouldn't know how to handle cow critters any more, Lord. Neither would the rest of us." He glanced at Riley sharply. "You need us?"

"I sure do."

"We'll see." Kehoe considered the problem. "From the Fork? They won't let you drive down the main trail."

Riley shrugged. "I know that. Otherwise I couldn't afford those cattle. I'm going to bring them over the Swell."

Kehoe was startled. "The hell you are!" Then he added, "Ain't water enough for a hundred head through there—not generally."

They were silent then for several minutes, huddling over the small blaze. The rain continued to fall, and Riley stole a glance at Kehoe's haggard cheeks. "You've had a rough time," he said abruptly.

Kehoe nodded. "We have. You were right to get out of it, Riley. The old days are gone."

He stood up and threw the remainder of his coffee on the ground. "I'll pass the word up on the Swell. If you can find water, you'll get through."

"This rain will help—and we've had a wet spring."

Kehoe handed him a slip of paper on which were scrawled three addresses. "If you need us, write to all three. One of them will get us."

"Kehoe?"

"Yeah."

"Stay out of Rimrock. That sheriff is too smart. He's a slow-moving Swede, and no youngster, but he was born canny."

Riley walked back to the house and stood there for a few minutes, mentally following Kehoe along the trail into the canyon. Kehoe had called him "Lord," a nickname he had given him back along the trail, short for Gaylord, but an old joke, resulting from the time in San Francisco when Riley had tried on a top hat. After that for quite some time they had called him "Lord Riley."

He fell into his bed and was instantly asleep, and when Cruz rolled out of bed half an hour later, Riley did not hear him.

The Mexican went outside in the growing light and studied the tracks. A few pieces of mud had fallen from the horse's shoes near the lean-to, and he picked them up and tossed them away. Then he got the horses saddled and led them several times over the tracks left by the stranger's horse.

Cruz had his own brand of loyalty. He rode for the brand, but even more for the man who owned it, and there had been a time, long ago and south of the border . . . Well, who can say what a man will not do in his youth?

The sun had not yet cleared the mountains behind the heavy gray clouds when they rode into Trail Canyon and began the devious ride toward the Dandy Crossing of the Colorado.

Darby Lewis remained behind to look after the saddle stock and to continue the work around the ranch house. He did not much like being alone, for he was by nature a gregarious man, yet he preferred being alone to the ride that lay before the others. And not for a minute did Darby Lewis believe they would return with cattle.

Coker Beaman was loafing in a saloon at Spanish Fork when Gaylord Riley found him. He walked to the bar with Cruz and ordered a drink, glancing at Beaman. The man had a bottle in front of him and there was a disgusted look on his face.

Riley glanced at him again. "You look like you were clouding up for a storm," he said mildly. "Let me buy you a drink."

Beaman indicated the bottle. "I've already had too many, and I never knew anybody to drink himself out of a hole."

"My name is Riley." He thrust out a hand. "What seems to be the trouble?"

The man shook Riley's hand. "Beaman here. Unless you're a cowhand hunting a job you couldn't help me; in fact, you couldn't help me unless you were ten cowhands heading for Kansas."

Riley chuckled. "I counted myself up a couple of times and I run short of ten. You sound like a man with cows to move."

"Nearly three thousand head," Beaman explained woefully. "I figured to make a drive from Oregon to Kansas and make a lot of money. After all, they were driving cows from Texas, why not from Oregon?"

"You'll have to admit," Riley suggested cautiously, "that it's a mite farther."

"Somewhat." Beaman did fill his glass. "This is a lot bigger country than I figured it was. I've got an uncle, a doctor, who lives down south of here. I figured to make myself a stake and go visit him."

"I've seen him . . . down to Rimrock. That is, if he's the same Doc Beaman."

"There can't be two of them in Rimrock," Beaman agreed. "My favorite uncle—in fact, he's my only uncle. Now I won't get to see him."

"You can ride down there," Riley suggested.

Beaman tasted his drink. "I'm a man with cattle," he said, "and no place to go. I can't find any hands who will drive through Sioux country, and I can't move the cows south because of the farmers. I wouldn't go back across that desert for anything under the sun, and there's nothing but mountains to the north, and while I sit here those damn cows are eating me out of all the cash I've got. I had to *rent* pasture, and by the time the week is out, I'll have to rent more."

He lowered his voice. "If I had a good horse I'd ride the hell out of here."

Riley tossed off his drink. "I've got a good horse," he said quietly, "and we might make a deal on the cattle."

Beaman laughed without humor. "Friend," he said, "I wouldn't wish it on you, but the grass is about gone from the pasture where I've been holding those cattle. It's going to cost me a dollar a head per month to graze them on the only pasture close by. That's close to three thousand dollars—and I pay in advance. Mister, I'm in trouble."

He filled his glass again. "They've got me over a barrel here, and they know it. First thing you know, they'll have those cattle, they'll have my shirt, and I'll be walking out of here afoot wondering what hit me."

He looked at Riley again. "Did you ever try doing business with a Mormon farmer? He's sharper than a Scotsman, and he'd trade a New England Yankee right out of his teeth."

Riley reached inside of his coat and drew out a folded sheet of paper. He spread it carefully on the bar and took up a pen that lay beside an inkwell at the corner of the bar where the bartender had been working on his accounts.

"Write me out a bill of sale," he said, "at your lowest price, and I'll buy your cattle right now, for cash."

Beaman turned his head and stared at him. "Now just a minute," he said. "I've got nearly three thousand head out there, and a lot of money invested in them."

"You've got three thousand head that you're about to lose," Riley replied coolly, "and I've got the money to buy them."

"Buying them," he lied, "is an idea I've just come on. I was figuring on buying myself a place around here. I may change my mind at any minute. In fact, if my wife hears about this she'll blow up. You know how women are."

Coker Beaman wet his lips with his tongue. The pasture where he had been holding the cattle was down to the roots now, and soon the cattle would be fighting the fences to get out. If he moved them he had to come up with three thousand dollars—which he did not have—before he could take them to fresh pasture.

"I've got nearly twenty thousand dollars in those cattle," he said.

"That isn't the point," Riley said mildly. "How much will you have tomorrow? Or the day after?"

He straightened up from the bar and reached for the sheet of paper. Beaman put a hand on it. "Wait."

"I'll give you three thousand dollars," Riley said, "right here—now—in gold."

"*What?*" Beaman almost screamed the word.

"*Three* thousand? Why, I'd be losing seventeen, eighteen thousand dollars! Are you crazy?"

"No—you were, when you started this drive without checking your facts." Riley started to button his coat. "I've got to be leaving. My wife is waiting, and—"

"Hold on—just a minute now. Let me think."

"About what? If I buy your cattle you'll have three thousand dollars in gold. If I don't buy them you're going to lose them and have nothing. What's there to think about?"

Beaman looked at him with disgust. "You're worse than those Mormons," he said. "You sure grind a man."

"I'm not grinding you," Riley said. "I'm offering you a way out." He turned to Cruz. "See if my wife is out there. If she's left the store, she'll be mighty impatient."

Cruz came back after a minute, his face grave. "I do not see her," he said, "but no doubt she is anxiously waiting."

"Now or never." Riley put the money belt Cruz carried on the bar. "There it is."

Beaman mopped a hand across his face, then opened the money belt. The shining gold pieces were there. He counted them, hesitated, then scratched his name on the bill of sale.

"You"—Riley indicated the bartender—"will you sign this as a witness?"

The bartender did so, and Riley shoved the change from ten dollars back to him. "Buy yourself a cigar," he said.

He thrust out a hand to Beaman. "Better luck next time," he said.

Out on the street, Cruz looked at him. "The señor is not married."

"You know, I thought about that, but it seemed to me I had a wife waiting for me somewhere, and the chances are she would be against this deal."

"Especially," Cruz said mildly, "as two men cannot drive three thousand head of cattle." His black eyes were interested, faintly amused. "What are you going to do with them?" But Riley did not answer.

At the trading post they replenished their supplies, then turned toward the pasture where the cattle were held.

It was a large, fenced area against a bluff, and when they rode up two men awaited them. A big bearded man in a black coat rode out to meet them, and Riley rode his horse slowly toward the two, then drew up.

"How are you, gentlemen? Something I can do for you?"

"You're Riley? You bought these cattle?"

"That I did."

"My land lies to the south, and not one head of cattle will cross my land . . . do you understand?"

"Sure." He smiled. "They won't come anywhere near your land. I shall be driving east."

"*East?* Then you are more of a fool than I suspected. There is a Sioux outbreak in Wyoming. Anyway"—and there was obvious satisfaction in his tone—"you'll find no cowhands. You can't move that herd without hands, or without a cavvy."

Riley merely lifted a hand in farewell and, opening the gate, allowed the cattle to drift out, with Cruz pushing them a little. As the grass was gone in the fenced pasture, the cattle were only too pleased to leave it. A few hundred yards off to one side, the two riders watched.

To the east there was open country with no fenced areas or tilled fields, and there was sparse grass. For that matter, there were few fenced areas to the south, and it was obvious that some of the local people had hoped to have those cattle for themselves, and no doubt still expected to get them.

Slowly, the herd strung out. Riley rode a good horse, and he needed it, for here and there a steer started for wider pastures to right or left, and both he and Cruz were hard put to keep the herd pointed, roughly at least, toward the wide spaces.

The herd had moved scarcely a mile when suddenly a rider emerged from a draw and fell in on the opposite side of the herd. There was a flurry of dust and two more riders appeared. Riley saw Cruz standing in his saddle to stare at them, but they worked steadily, ignoring him. The herd moved east and a little south, following the banks of the stream.

The two men to whom Riley had talked were now standing in their own stirrups, staring at the strange riders as if unwilling to believe what they were seeing.

The herd moved on steadily, falling easily into the movements of the drive, for they had been driven here from Oregon and were well broken to the trail. A big Durham cow had moved into the lead, and she stayed there.

At dusk, several miles out from Spanish Fork, they suddenly saw a thin column of smoke ahead of them, and one of the strange riders moved to the point and began to swing the herd.

Cruz, who had ceased to be astonished, glanced toward the fire as they drew near. Nearby was a cavvy of at least sixty horses, and while there was no chuck wagon, this was obviously a trail-drive camp. Cruz waited for Riley as he came around the herd to join him, and the two of them rode off toward the fire.

A slight man with a narrow, tough face was drinking coffee at the fire. "Riley?" he asked. "I'm *segundo*. Everything all right?"

"Couldn't be better."

"Me an' the boys will ride night guard," he said. "You'll have company, come daylight."

"Thanks."

Cruz accepted the plate of beans and beef that was handed him, and glanced quickly at Riley. But Riley had settled down to eat, and Cruz, with a shrug, did likewise.

Where the camp had been made the stream ran clear, and tall trees were close about. Riley liked the crackle of the fire, and the smell of woodsmoke. The coffee was good, and the grub even better. Occasionally a rider rode up to the fire, drank a cup of coffee, and rode away.

At daylight the herd was moving again, and from out of nowhere a dozen riders had appeared, all top hands, judging by the way they handled themselves and the herd. And so it went as the herd headed south from Castlegate, finally making the swing on the fifth day out.

From time to time a new rider would appear and there would be a brief conference, and then the herd would change its direction. Each change led them to water, though there was little enough, in any case. Often there were just pools from the rain, and occasionally a seep or spring. Sometimes there were low places in the river beds where water remained.

Once Cruz joined Riley to watch the herd amble past. "They look good, *amigo*," he said. "We have been fortunate."

"The rain saved us—and the other rains before that. It has been a wet spring, and there was snow left from the winter. Ordinarily you couldn't bring a dozen horses the way we will be riding, and to bring a herd of cattle would be out of the question."

"Especially," Cruz added dryly, "with only two cowhands."

Riley grinned at him. "Pays to have friends."

Cruz hesitated, and then he said, "I have heard of the Outlaw Trail, *amigo* . . . is this it?"

"Part of it. Canada to Mexico, right down the backbone of the country it goes, with stations all along the route. The Hole-in-the-Wall or Jackson's Hole in Wyoming, Brown's Hole at the corner of Wyoming, Colorado, and Utah; and Robber's Roost in Utah. Down in Arizona there is Horse Thief Valley near Prescott, and the Sulphur Springs Valley east of Tucson. Over in New Mexico there's a station near Alma, and away up in Montana there's one near Landusky, and another in the Crazy Mountains.

"Up Montana way somebody steals some cattle and they push them into the Outlaw Trail. A rancher on the trail pushes the 'strays' south, and the others do the same. Actually, nobody is stealing except the man who sells them. The others are just moving strays off their places. Only those Montana cows are finally sold in Mexico, or maybe in Arizona or Texas."

He indicated the hands driving the cattle. "They're just pushing them south to get them off their range, and day after tomorrow we'll have a new set of hands—maybe even a new cavvy."

When Cruz had ridden away, Gaylord Riley watched the drag of the herd drift by. His future rode with this herd; but more than that, the futures of the men who had given him his chance to amount to something in the world. Everything depended on getting the herd through . . . everything. And he was not at all reassured by the good start they had made, for the roughest, driest part of the trail lay ahead.

All he owned lay with that herd. True, there was money in the bank, money needed to carry him over until he had cattle to sell, but it was little enough, and he would find no such bargain as this herd. Not again.

Nor was it of himself alone that he thought, for the men who had given him his chance deserved a chance of their own. Mistakes they had made, just as he had made his, but they were not bad men, and the time was coming when they must end their riding. They would need a place, a place that was home.

There is always that within man, as deeply seated as is the desire to wander—the desire for a home, for a place that belongs to oneself, a shelter away from the world.

His own home would be here among these fantastic canyons, these towering spires. Around him would be the ruins left by those others who had come from no man knew where, built their houses in the hollows up the cliff walls, and had planned to stay—had, indeed, stayed for a long time. And then they had gone . . . vanished . . . to where?

Nor were they the first men who had come to this lonely land, for the strange paintings on the walls could not all have been of their making. What of the pictures he had seen not far from Spanish Fork—pictures of strange llama-like beasts of burden and their drivers, near the remains of what may have been an ancient mine? What people were those? What manner of beasts did they drive?

He was thinking of these things when a rider drew up near him. "We'll need beef. Is it all right to cut one out?"

Riley laughed. "Did you ever ask before?"

The rider was one-armed, Riley saw as he turned away. The fellow shot him an amused look. "Not often," he said, chuckling, "not very often."

NINE

Day after day the drive rolled southward under its hovering cloud of dust, south toward the five towering peaks of the Henrys, across the Dirty Devil, across the forty miles of parched desert that lay beyond. On across the Maidenwater Sands, and down the long arroyo of the Trachyte to Dandy Crossing, on the Colorado.

When Gaylord Riley and Jim Colburn, pointing the drive, reached the Crossing, Cass Hite walked out to meet them.

"Howdy, Cass!" Riley said. "Had many visitors lately?"

Hite came up to him, and spoke in a low tone, knowing how well sound carried in that rocky land.

"We never have many visitors, an' you damn well know it," he said pleasantly. "This here is about the loneliest place there is, unless it's that ranch site you picked.

"One thing, though. There's been a gent up on the mesa with a glass, a-watchin' for somebody. I'd not say it was for you exactly, but he showed up right after you went through, and he's been up there ever since."

The Colorado at this point described a large bend like a letter C with the open side toward the east. Dandy Crossing, and the "town" named for Hite, lay at the top of the C, the easternmost point, while within the bend was a mesa, roughly a thousand feet higher than the Crossing itself.

From up there a man with good glasses could watch not only the Crossing, but the approach to it along the canyon of the Trachyte.

"What do you think, Riley?" Colburn asked.

"Could be somebody layin' for you."

"More'n likely."

"You've got to go back, Jim. If that's a posse up there, they'd have you trapped. There's no other crossing in a good many miles downstream, and nothing up the river. If they're waiting for you over there, you'd never have a chance."

"We'll see you across the river, boy. From there on you'll be on your own."

"Riley," Hite suggested, "if you need he'p, I've a couple of loafers you can have. They owe me, and if I say they work for you, they dasn't say no."

"Send them along. I'll promise them three days' work. If they shape up, I can use them longer. Meanwhile," Riley added, "keep your eyes open for good men. I'd like to hire two more, full time."

"I'll shake hands now," Colburn said, "because when your cattle are across the river we'll take out for the faraway hills. Any posse hunting us is going to see plenty of dust and country."

For two weeks after the drive ended, Riley had no time for anything. When the cattle were turned into the basin, the branding was begun. There had been no time even to run a trail brand on the herd before leaving Spanish Fork.

The smoke of branding fires was in his nostrils, mingled with the smell of burning hair and dust. Only at night under the stars could he be free of it, and smell the soft wind, the cedars, and the sage.

It was hot, grueling work, with no let-up, but Cruz was a fast and a hard worker, a good roper, and a fine horseman. Darby

Lewis knew his business and worked without lost motion, but even so the job went slowly.

On the first day of the third week, Cruz rode over to Riley. "Rider coming, *amigo*. A stranger."

Riley straightened up from the branding fire and wiped the sweat from his face, then moved a hand back to slide the thong from his six-shooter.

The rider came on, riding a lineback dun and leading two pack horses that looked like good stock. He was a tall man wearing a buckskin shirt and a battered black hat. He drew up alongside the fire. "Riley? Cass Hite, down to Dandy Crossin', said you were needin' a hand."

"If you can ride an' rope, you're hired. Thirty a month an' found."

The man stepped down from the saddle, and he stood two inches taller than Riley's six-one. He squatted on his heels and picked up the coffeepot. "Soon as I get myself a cup of coffee, I'll be workin'," he said. "My name is Tell Sackett."

Riley had started to turn away, but he glanced back over his shoulder. "Sackett? Are you kin to the Sacketts of Mora?"

"Brother."

"Heard of them . . . like what I heard."

Together they plunged into the work. Cruz and Lewis now worked as a team, and Sackett worked with Riley. The new hand was fast and sure with a rope, and he had three good horses.

The day began at three A.M., when they rolled out in the cold, fired up, ate a fast breakfast, and by daylight usually had a rope on a cow. With the cavvy brought down the trail and supplied by the rustlers from the San Rafael Swell, Riley now had sixty-six horses in his corrals, and they were needed. Each man used three to four horses every day. The horses were 1,000 to 1,150 pounds as a rule, running heavier than Texas cow horses, and they had good, hard hoofs. Whatever shoeing was done the hands did themselves, using a rasp and then tacking on the shoe. No fire was needed, and no time wasted.

Where plenty of cattle had been caught up, two men did the roping and two the branding.

Twice, Gaylord Riley came upon tracks on the range, and once he caught a flash of sunlight from field glasses as somebody watched from a butte bordering the basin.

Each night they rode into camp dead tired, rarely returning to the house on the plateau, but camping among the cedars close to the basin and their work.

Strat Spooner rode into Rimrock shortly after nightfall. He rode directly to the Hardcastle saloon and swung down from the saddle. Across the street Sampson McCarty was closing his door, about to lock up for the night. He turned his head at the sound of the horse, and watched Spooner dismount.

It had been weeks since he had seen the big gunman in town, and both man and horse looked beat. Standing in the shadows, McCarty watched Spooner as he stepped up on the board walk. The saloon door opened and Hardcastle came out. The two stood talking in low tones.

Across the street there was a slight movement in the shadows, and McCarty strained his eyes to see a bulky figure loitering in front of the store. When the gunman mounted his horse to go on to the livery stable, McCarty saw the man emerge from the shadows and stroll toward the restaurant. It was Sheriff Larsen.

Neither McCarty nor Larsen had been in a position to hear what it was that Spooner had to say, and which Hardcastle was obviously anxious to hear.

In that conversation Spooner wasted no time. "Riley's back. Brought in a herd of mixed stuff, Shorthorns and white-faces, less than half of them branded so far. He has three hands riding for him, Cruz and Lewis and some drifter he picked up. They worked together most of the time, so I think your time is now."

Hardcastle took a handful of coins from his pocket, all of them gold. He handed them to Spooner, then added another.

"That's a bonus, Strat. You've done a good job. Now get some sleep."

Sampson McCarty walked on to the restaurant and joined Larsen. "I see Spooner is back in town."

"I see."

"Something's in the wind, Ed. What is it? What's going to happen?"

"Maybe . . . maybe nothing. I do not know."

McCarty knew from previous experience that when Larsen would not talk there was no use trying to get anything from him. He glanced around the room. "I haven't seen young Riley in town lately."

"No."

Just then Dan Shattuck opened the door for Marie and they entered the room, speaking to first one and then another. McCarty, who was at heart a romantic, noted the quick look around by Marie, and her evident disappointment.

"Somebody else," he commented to Larsen, "misses our friend Riley."

Larsen did not reply, and McCarty's eyes followed the sheriff's toward Spooner, who was staring at Marie. The expression in his eyes was both insolent and somehow possessive.

Dan Shattuck looked up and Spooner's eyes swung away, but not so quickly that Shattuck did not notice. McCarty saw the rancher's face darken with anger, but at a whispered word from Marie he turned his attention to her.

McCarty reviewed the situation in his mind and liked none of it. News there would be, and he was interested in news, but this situation looked like news of a kind he could do without. There were too many elements, too many threads . . . and some of those whom he both liked and respected were sure to be hurt.

Pico entered, and crossed to Shattuck's table and joined him. The big Mexican had been almost a member of Shattuck's family for many years, since long before Marie was born. It was well known in the community that Pico had long considered himself a sort of guardian for Marie.

Shattuck said something to Pico, and Marie seemed to be protesting. Pico's eyes lifted, and across the room they met the eyes of Strat Spooner, but the big gunman merely gave the Mexican a taunting smile and looked away.

McCarty was puzzled over Spooner's change of attitude. He had been around town for some time, but he had always been careful, had avoided contact with the people of the town, and had rarely left Hardcastle's saloon unless on some errand for Hardcastle. Now he seemed almost to invite trouble.

Strat Spooner's manner, the whispers of impending trouble for Shattuck, and the mysterious drifters who kept passing through town or reappearing in town worried McCarty. He was a friendly man, and the people of Rimrock he counted as his friends, yet even Larsen, under his placid exterior, was obviously worried.

Larsen had been going about more. He seemed never to sleep, and there were few evenings now when he was not dropping into the restaurant or one of the saloons. He was present, without fail, when Shattuck came into town, though he only watched and said nothing.

Several days passed after this evening in the restaurant, and McCarty was making up his paper. Suddenly a shadow fell across his window, and the door opened. It was Gaylord Riley.

He bought a newspaper, chatted a bit, then stepped outside. What happened then, McCarty observed with interest. Peg Oliver walked by and cut Riley dead. Eyes straight to the front, chin lifted, she walked right by him.

Riley stood there, his mouth opened to speak, but she kept on walking. Astonished, he shuffled the paper in his hands, then turned and walked toward the restaurant.

McCarty hesitated, glanced at the paper before him, and hurriedly took off his apron and his eyeshade. The paper could wait. He had a hunch he was going to learn something. He stepped out on the street, hastily shrugging into his coat.

He was in time to see Riley stopped by Sheriff Larsen, and as he approached he overheard what was said.

"Are you puying cows?"

"When I can find them . . . white-face or Shorthorn."

"I did nodt t'ink dere was so many aroundt."

"There aren't many."

"Do you haff pills of sale?"

Gaylord Riley slanted a sharp look at the Swede's bland face. "Sure . . . what are you getting at?"

"Do you mindt if I come oudt and look dem over?"

Riley felt his neck getting hot, and he was suddenly aware that all movement on the street had stopped. "Any time, Sheriff, any time at all."

Riley turned sharply away, and as he did so he saw Desloge. The gunman was seated on a bench before the saloon, and as their eyes met Desloge slowly, significantly, closed one eye.

Riley's anger rose, but he started on toward the restaurant, when Hardcastle stopped him. "Anything I can do," Hardcastle said, "you come to me."

Riley stopped abruptly. "What do you mean? How could you help me?"

Hardcastle shrugged. "I don't believe it for one minute, but the word's gone around town—Shattuck is losing cattle and blaming you."

"To hell with him!" Riley brushed by him and went to the restaurant.

At that hour it was almost deserted. The girl who took his order did not smile—she simply took the order and walked away. When his food was placed before him it was almost thrown upon the table.

Angrily he started to rise, but he was hungry, and there was no place else in town where a man could eat. He relaxed, and began to eat. It was then that McCarty came in.

"Mind if I sit down?"

Riley looked up with relief. "Glad to have you, but the way people are treating me, I don't know whether you should or not."

"I'll chance it." McCarty ordered his own supper and sat back, lighting his pipe. "Shattuck is missing cattle."

"So he blames me?" Riley said bitterly. "I've got plenty of cattle of my own."

"Who else would dare take them?" McCarty asked mildly. "There simply aren't any others anywhere in the country around. Nobody can understand where you got all those cattle you say you have."

"I bought that herd in Spanish Fork."

McCarty shrugged. "Understand me, I am not saying this, and it was I who told you of that herd, but some say there never was such a herd, and if there was there would be no way of getting it down, not from there to here."

He had brought that herd down over the Outlaw Trail, and few even knew of that trail's existence. The drivers who brought it down for him were themselves outlaws.

"I bought it from Doc Beaman's nephew—that doctor here in town."

McCarty looked up sharply. "Have you told anybody that? If you haven't, don't. Coker Beaman was found two weeks ago, shot dead beside the trail. He had been murdered and robbed."

Gaylord Riley suddenly stared at the food before him, his appetite gone. Within him arose a feeling of desperation. Was he to have no chance? Was this to be the end of all he hoped for?

"I didn't kill him. I bought the herd from him, and I have a bill of sale for it. I paid him in gold coin."

"Doc thought a lot of that boy. He's stirring up the law to find the killer."

"I hope they do find him." Riley sat back in his chair, trying to think the problem through.

He was a stranger here, a man without friends, a man with no history he dared to repeat. Nor could he call anyone as witnesses, for his friends were outlaws who dared not come in; and even if they did, their word would not be accepted.

"You'd better eat," McCarty suggested. "I think you're going to need it."

Riley knew it was unlikely that anyone would believe he had brought his herd of cattle through the rough, dry country where ordinarily two or three men on horseback were lucky to find enough water. And the men who knew anything about that country were few indeed, and unlikely to want to appear. Several were Mormons, hiding out for reasons best known to themselves, hard-working men who had found safety in the remote mountains of the Roost country.

He felt suddenly sick. He stared bleakly across the room. He could give it all up and run. He could ride back to Dandy Crossing, swim the Colorado, and head for the Roost. There probably had not been one night when, half-consciously, the outfit had not waited, expecting him to come. It was hard for an outlaw to make it on the outside. Their futures as well as his own were at stake here, and he had cattle and a ranch, and a home being built.

"If anybody comes hunting me," Riley said, "you tell them they won't have to look far. I'll be out there in the Sweet Alice Hills, or I'll be here. If they want to talk, I'll talk; but if they come hunting trouble, they'll get a belly full of it."

McCarty's eyes warmed. "Good lad," he said quietly. "Stay with it, and I'll stay with you—as much as a man can."

TEN

Martin Hardcastle rolled the cigar in his lips and considered the situation with pleasure. From their hide-out in the Blues his men had struck swiftly at the Shattuck herds. They had stolen only a few cattle at first, and they had left not too clear a trail—a trail that led into the broken canyon country beyond which lay the Sweet Alice Hills.

A few nights later, they had struck again, and to make it not too obvious, they had swept up a few Boxed O cattle at the same time.

Hardcastle himself had helped to foment the talk about the white-face cattle; after all, where could Gaylord Riley get such cattle when Shattuck would not sell? And why would any honest man choose to live in such a remote place?

Hardcastle knew from experience that most people love to talk, and like to repeat what they have heard. Trouble is born of rumor, and nine people out of ten will repeat a rumor—consciously or unconsciously adding their bit. Out of those rumors had come Peg Oliver's attitude, Larsen's questions, and McCarty's sympathy.

Hardcastle was bidding for a cattle war out of which he

would not only have his revenge against Dan Shattuck, but a profit in sweeping up the pieces. He would not be suspected, since he had nothing—apparently—to gain.

Riley was young and likely to be hot-headed. Dan Shattuck was stubborn and hot-headed himself. Hardcastle intended to see a gun battle between the two, and he did not care which man won. He knew nothing of Riley's skill with a gun.

Gaylord Riley had planned to remain over night in town, but now he decided against it. With two pack horses loaded with supplies, he took the trail to the hills. Behind him, but not too far behind, rode Desloge.

Desloge was too shrewd not to see what Hardcastle was bidding for, and was also too shrewd not to realize the whole affair would erupt into a shooting match of which he wanted no part. A bad man with a gun, Desloge had long since been aware that men get killed in gun battles, and that there is no telling who will die and who will survive. Bullets are indiscriminate, and he had no intention of dying at this stage of the game. Hence, what he wanted was quick cash and a quick ride out of the country.

He had an idea he would have that cash from Gaylord Riley.

The ranch was deserted when Riley rode into the yard. A note on the table told him that all three men had gone back to the basin to brand stock.

Riley stripped the horses of their packs and turned them into the corral; then he took in the articles purchased in Rimrock and arranged them on the shelves. Among other things he had bought five hundred rounds of ammunition.

He chuckled when he recalled the expression on the storekeeper's face when he had given his order. "*Five hundred rounds!* What are you expecting? A war?"

"Hate to have one come an' not be ready to take part," Riley had replied. "Like goin' to a hangin' and forgettin' your rope."

He heard the horse walk into the yard, and turned quickly to the door. It was Desloge.

The outlaw drew up, smiling with his thin lips. "Like old times, ain't it, Riley?" he said.

"What do you mean? Old times? I never saw you but once in my life before, and I've no business with you."

"Well, now." Desloge was very sure of himself. He clasped his palms on the pommel and continued to smile, but there was no friendliness in his eyes. "That's as may be. S'posin' I was to go to Dan Shattuck with what I know? Or to that Swede sheriff?"

Riley's reaction was so swift that Desloge had no time to prepare, no time to resist. A swift blow knocked his hands loose from the pommel, then he was jerked from the saddle.

Desloge hit the ground with a thump, and Riley grabbed him by the collar with a short, twisting grip that set the outlaw to gagging. Jerking him to his knees while Desloge's hands clawed at his wrist, Riley slapped him three times across the face, ringing blows that left streaks where they landed. Then he threw Desloge to the ground and stepped back.

"You've got a gun," he said coolly. "All you've got to lose is your life."

Desloge lay where he had fallen, his stomach tight with fear. Nothing had gone as he had planned. He had been sure his threats would frighten Riley into a pay-off, and he knew Riley had the money. He had planned to suggest that for a thousand dollars he would ride clear out of the country, but now he had a sickening realization he would be lucky to get out alive. He had expected a half-frightened boy. He had cornered a mountain lobo.

"All I wanted," he said, and his voice was shaking, "was a road stake. Say a hundred dollars?" Riley had shaken his confidence—nine hundred dollars' worth.

"Ride out the way you rode in," Riley replied, "and be glad you're able. And stay away from Rimrock. If I hear one word of this I'll hunt you down and hang your pelt on the nearest tree."

Desloge struggled to his feet, careful to keep his hands free of his gun. Even more carefully he climbed into his saddle. As he settled down and started to turn his horse, four men rode into the ranch yard. Three rode in from the basin: Tell Sackett, Darby Lewis, and Cruz. The fourth was a hard-faced man with white hair, a stranger to the other three.

"Take a good look," the white-haired man advised them, "then you'll be able to swear that man rode away from here, and what he looked like. Get that?"

And then the white-haired man turned his horse and rode away, following Desloge.

Forty minutes later Desloge slowed his running horse to walk him down a slope near a butte.

It was sundown, and the shadows were long. Odd, how much the shadows added to the fearsomeness of this wild land. Down there, near the brush . . . that rock looked like a man on a horse.

Desloge rode on, and the rock moved. It not only looked like a man on a horse; it *was* a man on a horse, and he knew the man. A man with white hair and a seamed brown face.

And in that instant, Desloge knew he was going to die.

He had killed men, but he had never known how it felt to be about to die. He knew now.

"Couldn't let him live honest, could you?" There was no anger in the man's voice. "Your kind could never do that. He put fear into you, and you'd ride away, but sooner or later you'd talk. You would spoil something fine."

Desloge struggled for words. He wanted to beg, but he had a feeling it would be useless. He wanted to deny what the man said, but he would be lying; and he felt that now was not a time to lie.

"I'll ride," he said at last. "I won't even stop for my warbag. I'll just keep going."

"You've killed men. You've got a gun."

It had grown dark, but then an early moon had brought more light. Desloge cleared his throat. He started to speak, and then he thought he saw his chance. He touched his horse with a spur and swept his hand down for his gun as the horse leaped.

The gun cleared the holster. He felt a bursting sense of

triumph as his gun swept up, then down on its target. He'd show that old—

He ran into something in the darkness. Something white-hot that burned all the way through him and somehow started him floating toward the ground. He felt himself hit and roll over; and then he was looking up at the moon and he was dead.

It was Sheriff Ed Larsen who found the body.

He was not surprised. Desloge had come to the sort of end such men as Desloge all come to sooner or later, led to it in many cases by their very attempt to escape it.

Nor was it by accident that he found the body, for he had been trailing Desloge and had hoped to catch him before he reached Riley's ranch.

Larsen, who had seen many men die, was never astonished by death. Desloge had had his chance. His gun lay where it had been jolted from his hand. He had been struck by only one bullet and there was almost no blood. Death in this case appeared singularly undramatic.

Despite his age, Larsen was a powerful man. He picked up the dead man and draped him over the empty saddle of his horse, then leading the horse, he returned to his own, took some piggin strings, and tied the body.

He turned back to go to Rimrock, but the Shattuck ranch was closer, and he went there.

There was dancing at the ranch. Marie came quickly to the door at the sound of the horses, and Larsen thought he detected disappointment in her eyes when she recognized him. He had dropped the reins of the dead man's horse back at the edge of the light.

"Gaylord Riley? He is not here?"

"Did you think he would be?" Shattuck had come to the door, followed by Oliver and two other men, Eustis and Bigelow. "In this house?"

Larsen glanced slyly at Marie. "I thought so," he said. "I thought he might be . . . around."

"What's the matter?"

"Feller killed . . . oudt by the buttes."

"Riley!" Eustis exclaimed. "By the Lord Harry, we've got him! Need a posse, Sheriff?"

"If you like, come. Dere will be no trouble, I t'ink."

"He has some men out there," Shattuck said, "but Lewis won't fight. Neither will Cruz. Not when he sees who it is."

"Cruz will fight," Pico interrupted. "He will die, if need be."

"Then we'll hang Cruz along with him," Eustis said angrily. "I've lost sixty, seventy head in the past two weeks."

Pico looked at him. "To hang Cruz will not be easy . . . nor to hang Riley. Men will die before either is hung."

Dan Shattuck glanced sharply at Pico. The Mexican was a shrewd judge of men, and he thought he detected a note of liking in his voice.

"You are not with us, Pico?"

"In this, I am with the sheriff. I think he will do what should be done. To talk of hanging is foolish."

"Stay here then, and be damned! We don't need you!" This was Eustis, who was a hot-head.

The men rushed to get their horses, and as Larsen and Pico stood together, waiting, they heard another horse slip away in the darkness.

Pico smiled . . . she had chosen well. The horse she had taken was a racing mare. It is good to be young and in love, he told himself. Like my own daughter she is, he thought, and I was afraid it would not come for her—the joy, and the hurt.

The mare ran, then trotted; ran and trotted, walked and ran again. Gaylord Riley heard the racing horse and was waiting on the trail in the moonlight when she appeared.

She drew up, swinging her horse broadside to him. "Riley, did you kill Desloge?"

"No."

"They believe you did. They're coming for you, Larsen and the ranchers!"

"All right!" he said calmly.

She almost cried with impatience. "Don't just stand there! You must get away. You can go to Dandy Crossing!"

"I'll wait for them."

She started to protest, then recognized the futility of it. "They'll not believe you," she said.

"I have wanted a home too long to run from it now. I shall stay." He indicated the house. "Go inside. I'll put your mare in the stable out of sight."

She was surprised at the neatness of the room, and she liked the way it was built. She looked around curiously. There were two doors, closed up now, doors obviously meant to lead to other rooms.

When he came into the house she was drinking coffee. She looked at him, so tall and strong; yet somehow so much alone, and her hands wanted to reach out to him.

"I have not thanked you," he said. And then he added, "When this is over, I should like to come calling."

He gestured around, not waiting for her reply. "This is only one room. There will be seven or eight. I shall build the house in the shape of an L, with the open side toward the south, I think. The setting sun is beautiful, but it can be hot.

"I want some old Spanish furniture, large, very comfortable, suitable for this house. And I want a garden out there." He motioned toward the south. "I have heard of flowers that do well at this altitude, and I shall send for as many as I can think of, or hear of."

They heard the sound of the horses on the hard trail, and on the rocks.

"When this is over," he said, "I shall want you here . . . always."

He was standing alone in the moonlight when the sheriff rode into the yard with the posse.

"Late riding, Sheriff," he said quietly, "but you're in good company. Or are you?"

"We want you for killing Desloge!" Eustis announced loudly. "Drop those gun belts!"

"*I* talk here," Larsen said sternly.

Dan Shattuck was a man honest with himself, if stubborn and opinionated, and he found himself admiring the cool courage of the young man who stood alone in the night, facing a hanging posse. There was no bravado in this young rancher, only a calmness, a certainty of himself.

"Did you see Desloge today?" Larsen asked.

"He was here."

"What for?"

"That's my business."

"It is my pusiness now. He has been killed."

"I didn't do it."

Eustis started to interrupt, but stopped at Larsen's lifted hand.

Cruz moved out of the darkness and took his place a few yards from Riley. Darby Lewis was just beyond him. Tell Sackett walked up and stood beside Riley, waiting.

"Come away from there, Darby!" Oliver said. "This isn't your fight!"

Surprisingly, Darby replied, "If you draw a gun, it is my fight," he said. "I ride for the brand."

Cruz spoke up, telling quietly of the strange man with white hair and his advice to them.

"A lie!" Eustis said.

Cruz looked at him. "Another time, señor, we will speak of that. I do not lie."

"He's right," Darby agreed. "Never saw the man before, but I'll read you this. He was nobody to mess with."

Sheriff Larsen believed them, Riley was sure of that. There was no telling what Shattuck believed, but Eustis did not believe, nor did the others, except Oliver.

Larsen's gaze shifted to Sackett. "You I do not know."

"I'm Tell Sackett," the man replied, "and I ride for the brand—or shoot for it."

Sackett . . . several pairs of eyes turned to look again, for it was a known name.

"One question," Larsen said. He seemed ready to leave. "Had you ever seen Desloge before?"

"Yes . . . once before, and only once. He was a thief and a cow rustler. I ordered him off the place."

"I t'ink dat concludes our pusiness," Larsen said. "We go back to town."

"Now, see here!" Eustis protested.

"We go back to town," Larsen repeated.

Dan Shattuck was strangely silent. Bigelow and the others looked to him for leadership, but he said nothing. Only once Larsen saw Shattuck's eyes stray toward the house, but whatever was in his mind remained unspoken.

Eustis alone objected. "Damn it, man! We came out here after a rustler, and I'll be damned if—"

"*I* keep the peace here," Larsen said. "You will ride back with us. You will go back freely, or as my prisoner."

"Well, I'll be damned if—"

"We go," Larsen said, and they went.

ELEVEN

Cruz and the others strolled away, and Gaylord Riley stood alone, staring into the night, listening to the fading sounds of the posse. So far, so good, but nothing had been changed— nothing had been changed in the least.

Only Larsen had stood between them and gunplay, and even he might not have averted it had not Dan Shattuck hung back. Why?

Turning toward the house, he saw the movement within, and suddenly he knew.

Shattuck knew or had guessed that Marie was here, and had the house been attacked, her presence would have been discovered. And no explanation would have prevented people from thinking the worst.

He went into the house and closed the door behind him, and Marie came quickly to him. "What you said before they came" —she caught his arm—"did you mean that?"

Miserably, he knew he had no right to involve her in what lay ahead, yet it was what he had wished to say, and the words, started from him as they had been, were nevertheless what he felt. But when he recalled Jim Colburn and the

82

others, a connection that sooner or later must be exposed, he hesitated.

She saw the hesitation, and misunderstood. Abruptly, her face pale, she pushed by him and started for the door.

"Please! Let me answer."

"You didn't mean it," she said. "You didn't mean it."

"I meant it," he insisted, "but I've no right. I—"

She ran out the door, and went to her horse, which Cruz was holding for her. Riley started after her, then stopped. For what was there to say? How could he ask her to share what he faced? His ranch was at least half owned by his outlaw friends, and it was to them he owed his first loyalty. And there was trouble coming, trouble that would split the Rimrock area wide open, and he would be a fool to ask her to join him in that. Especially when Dan Shattuck was on the other side.

A week passed, and then another. The branding went more slowly as they found fewer unbranded cattle. They had begun to know the terrain, and now each rider carried a running iron and branded any that needed it, wherever they could be found.

There was much to do besides the branding. They built a dozen small spreader dams on hillsides to spread out the runoff and give the water a chance to sink into the ground; and they built a bunkhouse. Fall would be coming with its cold winds, and winter with its snow. There was no need to build windbreaks, for they came naturally in this country of mesas, canyons, and jumbled heaps of boulders. From a meadow near a seep, Riley, helped by Sackett, cut several tons of hay.

Tell Sackett, the tall, quiet young man from Tennessee, used a scythe easily and with skill. The man cut the hay, stacked it for winter, and, knowing how cowhands hate to do manual labor, Riley took it on himself to cut wood for the winter. He rigged a stone-boat and hauled logs from wherever he found them. There were a number of deadfalls, trees that had fallen or had been blown down, and these he gathered first, to remove the danger of fire in the woods and to give what grass might come up a chance.

They saw no one, and they heard no news. None of them went near Rimrock, nor did any rider from the town or the other ranches approach them. Once, riding to Dandy Crossing after tobacco, Darby Lewis heard that Doc Beaman was talking up trouble over the death of his nephew, insisting that he had been murdered, his cattle stolen. Eustis was no longer even speaking to Larsen, and had banded together with Bigelow and some others to seek the sheriff's removal from office.

In the days that followed, Riley began his exploration of Dark Canyon. It was a gorge from fifteen hundred to two thousand feet deep, so narrow that for miles the sun never reached the bottom except at noon, when it was directly overhead. In some places scarcely a hundred feet wide, it ran from Elk Ridge, some miles east of the ranch, to the Colorado, where it ended as a mere slit in the rock wall.

Much of the canyon bottom was choked with a thick growth of trees and brush, dotted with pools of clear, cold water supplied by small streams trickling down from a number of springs higher up the canyon, as well as in the branch canyons. Here and there the pools were fairly deep, and were shaded with cottonwood, box elder, ash, and ferns. When sunlight touched the higher walls of the canyon it turned to amazing color the sandstone and limestone walls, stained by water, streaked by iron or salt. Only one trail led to the bottom, a dim trail used only by wild animals.

On one of his exploring trips in the canyon, Riley dismounted and walked ahead of his horse, allowing the animal to choose its own way. At times the inside stirrup scraped the wall as the horse edged past.

The walls towered immensely high above him. It was very still. Pausing, he listened, and beside him his horse listened, ears pricked.

Great boulders bulked among the trees; willows leaned over the still, cold pools. There was no sound but the faint trickle of

water and the hum of bees. When a rock fell, it only empha-
sized the stillness and solitude of the place.

Riley walked on, almost on tiptoe, bringing his own silence
to the silence of the canyon. If worse came to worst, he
thought, he would come here, he would hide out here.

For several miles he worked his way cautiously along the
bottom, finally leaving his horse at a small meadow among the
trees, where the grass was luxurious and green. That meadow,
he realized, could not be seen from above. The lower walls of
the canyon rose sheer, while up there they ran back steeply for
some distance, and as a consequence the best position one
could find for looking down into the canyon was well back from
the sheer edge.

Here, in the barren, rocky country of the southeastern
corner of Utah was a veritable Eden, a place so lovely and so
remote as to be unbelievable. And from above not a hint of it,
so far below.

Behind some cottonwoods and willows Riley found an over-
hang forming a good-sized cave, not too far from the meadow.
The floor of the cave was level, of smooth sand and rock. There
was a spring nearby that spilled water into a deep, shaded
pool.

He had discovered what he wanted . . . a hide-out where he
could retreat in case of trouble; a place where Colburn and the
others could hole up and still be close by.

But even while he explored the canyon, always in the back
of his mind there were thoughts of Marie.

Dan Shattuck said nothing to Marie on her return, waiting to
see if she would say anything herself, but she did not. That she
had suffered a shock was obvious; twice when passing her
bedroom door in the night, he was sure he heard her crying.

Alone in his own room, he stared dismally at the wall. He
had never known anything about women. His own marriage
had not been a success, and a good part of that had probably
been his own fault. Yet if it had done nothing else, it had given

him time to think and to respect the feelings of others. After his wife left him he had for a time acted the fool. Whether it was love for her or simply hurt feelings that made him do so, he never did understand, but after a while, there was no more of this.

He had often been lonely before Marie had come to live with him. She had changed his life in every way, and a welcome change it was. He was no longer lonely and rarely depressed, and he had somebody to think about other than himself.

Pico had helped. Pico understood women much better than he did, and he was ready to admit it—to himself at least. No matter what face he might put on for other people, he had never fooled himself.

Now he was losing cattle, and they were cattle he could ill afford to lose, but he said no more about it. There was more talk than ever, and he knew that all he had to do was speak a word and a group of self-appointed vigilantes would ride out to Dark Canyon and there would be a hanging.

Oddly enough, he who had been so sure was no longer so. He had gone to the ranch reluctantly, but he had gone; and had he not seen Marie's shadow against the curtain he might have led an attack. Once he realized she was there, he was helpless—if the others discovered her presence there, he knew the kind of talk there would be. They would not know, as he did, that she had raced there ahead of them to warn Riley. And talk could destroy her—and him, too, when it came to that; although that had not occurred to him at the moment.

He knew, too, that he would kill the first man who spoke against her, and it would not end with one killing. There were always more.

Marie still rode out, taking long rides across the high mesas, but she rarely rode toward Dark Canyon. Occasionally on those rides she saw the tracks of other riders.

One day she had ridden out across the mesa and, leaving the trail that descended into Cottonwood Draw and followed the creek back into the Blues, she held to the mesa itself and skirted the base of the Blues, planning to water at a spring under the rim of Maverick Point.

It was a wild and lonely country, but she rode with confidence. Never in all her rides had she encountered trouble, and there was small chance she would see anyone in this empty land.

She had discovered the spring several years before, and had never seen any tracks there but those of wild animals, but now as she slid her horse down into Hop Creek, which offered access to Cottonwood Draw near the spring, she suddenly smelled smoke.

Concealing her horse among the cedars, she worked her way along the bench above Cottonwood Draw until she could look down upon the spring.

Three men stood about a fire, and there were four horses. She did not see the fourth man until one of the others went to him with a cup. She lay there, watching them, knowing the man was ill.

But why were they here, in this lonely place?

Suddenly a voice was raised, and a man said, "The devil with what he wants! He'll die here. I say, take him to the kid's place!"

Voices were lowered then, and they talked for some time. At last the tallest one of the group mounted his horse and, taking great pains to cover all sign, he rode away. After a bit, she went back to her own horse and followed.

She lost him when she crossed Cottonwood Draw above their camp, but sighted him again on Maverick Mesa. She lost him again, then saw him riding along the Reef of Rocks, headed west. She was sure now—there was nothing over there but Riley's place until you came to Dandy Crossing. When they spoke of the "kid" they had to mean Riley. Taking another trail, she started for Rimrock.

She rode swiftly, thinking of the strange riders in the canyon, and of the wounded man, for she was sure he must have been wounded. She did not think about where she was riding, for she knew all of the trails very well; she had no wish now but to get back to the ranch, to be at home before her uncle began to worry. And it was already late.

Riding down to the banks of a small creek, she started to wade her horse through when she saw a rider sitting his horse in the middle of the trail. To right and left there was thick brush, and her only route lay straight ahead.

She looked again, trying to make out the features under the hat brim. She saw that the man was Strat Spooner, and suddenly she was frightened.

He stared at her, smiling a little, as her horse walked nearer. By his gaze she was made acutely conscious of her figure, of the way her breasts tautened the material of her blouse. She wished she were away from here, anywhere at all.

"You're quite a ways from home, Marie," he said, and his smile broadened. His eyes held a curious hard yet speculative glint. "And quite a woman, I'd say."

To ride on was to draw nearer to him, but to turn back meant to ride into wilder country, where there was nothing and nobody. She hadn't seen so much as a chipmunk in miles.

She started to ride around him but he swung his horse in front of hers, still smiling, a lazy, insolent smile.

"Are you going to get out of my way?"

"Ain't decided."

He rested his big hands on the pommel of the saddle and rolled his fresh cigarette in his teeth. She was mighty pretty, but if she kicked up a row he'd have to leave the country. He had seen what happened to men who molested women in the western country—there was nothing that brought action faster. If a man was lucky he would simply be hung; some had been burned.

If she kicked up a fuss . . . but would she? Maybe she was just waiting for a man like him. She was a high-stepping filly with quite a body under the clothes. He felt himself starting to sweat.

Marie Shattuck was in a quandary. She might try riding upstream or downstream in the water, but the creek was shadowed by willows and cottonwoods; and back there away from the trail it was now almost dark. Yet the longer she delayed the greater the danger.

Putting spurs to her horse, she started forward with a lunge, but Spooner was too quick and too ready. His big hand dropped to her wrist, and as her horse leaped forward she was dragged from the saddle.

Instantly, she swung her quirt. The leather lash whipped across his face, and involuntarily he jerked back. Even in the half-light she could see the livid streak where the quirt had struck him. With an oath, he lunged for her—and then a rope shot out of nowhere and Strat Spooner was jerked back off his feet into the water.

Wildly, he fought to throw off the rope, and struggled to get to his feet. The stranger's horse simply backed up, as any good roping horse would do, and Spooner sprawled in the water, cursing. He grabbed for his gun but it was gone, fallen from his holster when he had hit the water.

Marie recognized the rider at once. It was the tall man she had seen by the fire in the canyon. "Evenin', ma'am," he said gently. "This feller seems to need a mite of cooling off."

"Drown him for all I care!" she flared. Then she smiled. "I want to thank you. I don't know what I'd have done."

The black horse moved again, and Strat Spooner fell again, all sprawled out.

"Figured you'd best have an escort back to Rimrock, ma'am. I know Riley would be mighty put out if he knew a friend of his was in trouble."

"You're a friend of his?"

"Lord Riley? I should reckon." He turned his horse and dragged Spooner out on the far bank. He shook the rope loose and Spooner backed out of the loop.

"I'll kill you for this!" Spooner said.

"My, my! He surely does get wrought up, ma'am. Maybe what he needs is an evenin' walk."

Spurring his horse, he rode up alongside of Spooner's horse and slapped it lightly with the rope. The horse leaped away and Spooner broke into a torrent of curses.

Kehoe rode up beside her. "If you will permit me," he said politely, "I'll ride the rest of the way into town with you."

"Be careful. That was Strat Spooner back there."

"Heard of him."

"He's killed several men."

"He seemed mighty upset back there." Kehoe glanced at her. "Was he waitin' for you?"

"He might have been. I—I often ride this way." She paused, thinking about it. "Now that I remember, so does he. And not only when I ride out that way."

"Nothing out there to call a man."

Kehoe was puzzled. And then he did remember something. "Unless he's tied in with those men holed up over in the Blues. There's twenty or thirty men over there—gunhands, and such.

"You know the spring over east of the head of Indian Creek?" he went on. "They're holed up there, a pretty rough crowd. We stumbled on them one time—they didn't see us—and it was pretty obvious they were hiding out. I recognized one of them. A man named Gus Enloe—a wanted man down in the Nation."

She had heard the name somewhere.

By now they were at the edge of Rimrock. He drew up and half turned to go.

"Who are you? What shall I call you?" she asked.

"You mustn't call me anything, Miss Shattuck. Just forget about me. I know that Lord is very concerned about you . . . not that he has mentioned your name, because he wouldn't. But when I heard your horse crossing Cottonwood Draw, I followed on to see who you were, and then trailed you back toward town to make sure you got home all right."

"Thank you. . . . You called him 'Lord'?"

"Short for Gaylord—one time I saw him trying on a top hat and said he looked like a lord."

"You've known him long?"

Kehoe hesitated, and then he said quietly, "Yes, I have . . . long enough to know there isn't a better man anywhere, at any time; and if he's given a chance, he will make something of that ranch."

"They are saying he has stolen cattle."

"Lord? Not on your life."

"But he has cattle?"

"He bought that herd up Spanish Fork way, and drove it down over the Swell."

"But that's impossible!"

"No, it isn't. Most times it is, but if a man tries it after heavy rains, as he did, and if he has friends who tell him where the water is, then he can make it. And believe me, he made it. I'm one of the men who helped him."

"One of your friends was hurt."

"You noticed that? Yes, he is, and we're worried."

"Do you have anything—medicines, or like that?"

"Nothing," Kehoe said bitterly. "We haven't a damn thing, and he'll fight us if we try to take him to the kid's place—to Lord's. He's afraid he'll get him into trouble."

"It's a bullet wound?"

Kehoe knew he had gone too far not to trust her now; in fact, he had been trusting her all the way along. "Yes," he said.

"You wait here. I'll ride in and see what I can get."

She rode swiftly to the drugstore. She had several times helped to care for wounds, and knew very well what to get that the drugstore had in stock. She ordered quickly.

The druggist, a short, red-faced man named White, looked at her. "You had a shootin' yonder? To the ranch?"

"No . . . only Uncle Dan wanted to have these things on hand . . . with the rustlers, and all."

"Oh, sure! Liable to be some shootin', at that."

Then he scowled. "Say, come to think of it, Pico was in here and stocked up only last week. Durned near bought me out."

"Give the things to me anyway," she said impatiently. Every moment the man waited he was in danger, and he might begin to doubt her and just ride off. "And please hurry!"

"Well, if you say so," White grumbled, "but Pico, he bought

enough bandages and medicine and such-like to outfit a regiment. Seems a waste of—"

"Are you going to give me what I ordered or not?"

"Oh, sure!" Hastily, he wrapped up the package. "I surely didn't mean—"

She took the package and turned swiftly toward the door, brushing by the man who was coming in, not even noticing who it was.

Ed Larsen turned and looked after her. Now, how long had it been since Marie Shattuck had failed to speak to him? He walked to the counter.

"A dime's worth of hoarhound," he said. "I take to sweets," he explained. "Aboudt all dat's left for an old man."

"That Marie Shattuck," White said, shaking his head. "I never knew her to get mad before. She—"

Sheriff Ed Larsen was a patient man and a good listener, and tonight he listened, offering no comment until the end of what the druggist had to say.

"Some boy," he explained wisely. "Young girls get mighty fidgety at such times."

White's face cleared. "Oh, sure! Never thought of that!"

Larsen went outside and closed the door behind him, effectively cutting off the questions White would have. After all, it was a small town, and White would be curious. Also, there were very few eligible young men around, and Larsen did not wish to be subjected to White's speculations.

Marie was gone, leaving only the dust of her going to settle in the empty street.

"If I were to ride oudt," he said aloud, "I could get to the ranch aboudt suppertime. Seems to me Dan Shattuck eats late."

The more he thought of it, the more he thought it was a good idea. And it was not much of a ride, when a man considered the kind of cooking at Shattuck's ranch.

And no telling what a man might turn up—if he listened.

TWELVE

The dining room at Shattuck's ranch was a long, low room with heavy beams and a huge fireplace. Dan Shattuck was a man who liked to live well, and he had come to the frontier when living well was impossible.

Breakfast he ate with the hands, and at noonday he was usually on the range and ate a lunch, or he was at a chuck-wagon or a campfire. Supper he insisted on enjoying in the grand manner, at a table with a tablecloth, cut glass, and silver.

Partly, it was a matter of preference; but partly, too, it was for Marie's sake. This was the background a girl should have, he believed, the background of a stable home, of dignity, courtesy, and manner—but without stuffiness.

Of the visitors who came to his table, Sampson McCarty, Sheriff Larsen, Oliver, and Doc Beaman were welcome at any time. Sampson McCarty and Doc Beaman were both there tonight when Larsen rode in and was promptly invited to dinner.

Marie, who had changed quickly and hurried to the dining room for supper, came to the door just as the men were walking into the room, and she caught a thread of conversation as she entered.

". . . holdup at Casner Station. One of them, at least, was wounded. I believe it was the Colburn bunch."

Doc Beaman was a wiry little man, often rough, always impatient. For all of that, he was a good doctor, and the frontier was accustomed to roughness. Had he been easier to get along with, he might never have come west, for his professional training was far superior to the average doctor of his time.

He was impatient now. "Damn it, Larsen," he said testily, "when are you going to arrest that Riley? You know damn well he's a thief. And probably a murderer. I've heard he admits he got those cattle from Coker."

"Dere is no evidence of such a t'ing. Of stealing—Burrage, he tells me nearly four t'ousand dollar was drawn by Riley."

"We're all losing cattle," Oliver suggested mildly, "and we weren't before he came into the country. I will admit that's no evidence, but there it is."

McCarty helped himself to the roast beef and passed the plate to the sheriff. "I told him your nephew had those cattle at Spanish Fork, and I let him know they might be had for a bargain. You told me yourself he tried to get additional capital from you, Doc."

"Well, he didn't get it! Coker Beaman was always a fool about money. Throwing good money after bad! Why, he knew nothing about cattle! That boy jumped into one fool thing after another. Just the same, he was murdered. Murdered and robbed, and who knew he had that money? The only one who could have known was Riley."

"A dozen men might have known," McCarty suggested. "Doc, if you operated on your patients with as little evidence as you're using to convict Riley, you'd have a lot of dead men on your hands."

"Operation—that's what's needed. That's just what's needed! An operation with a rope!"

"He's a hard worker," Shattuck said suddenly. "When we were out there that night, I noticed it. He's done a lot of work. A man like that doesn't steal."

Marie glanced at him quickly, gratefully, and he was glad he had said it, even if he was not quite sure of what he said. Work had been done—he had begun to notice that before they reached the ranch. They had crossed a small wash and he had seen a dam holding back a little water. Later he had seen a spreader dam on a slope. He had never built such a thing himself, but he had heard of them. Then the house, the corrals . . . and he knew the kind of rawhide building rustlers did. They threw together a shack, never expecting to be around very much. Riley's house was of logs—and built to take additions. Riley might be a thief, but if he was he intended to be among them for a long time.

"Eustis is right!" Beaman declared. "If the sheriff here doesn't see fit to act, then we must band together and do it ourselves!"

Larsen buttered a thick slice of bread, bit off a piece, and chewed it with appreciation. Whatever else might be said of Shattuck, he certainly had the best butter in the country.

"When dere is acting to do," he said cheerfully, "I shall do it." He lifted his old blue eyes and looked across the table at Doc. "And if Eustis or anybody else moves against anybody, I shall arrest him, and I shall see him convicted of whatever crime is committed." Larsen smiled. "That includes you, Doctor."

There was no anger in his voice, not even a ring of authority, simply the calm statement of fact, but Doc Beaman had no doubts. Ed Larsen would do exactly as he said.

When the others rose to go into Dan Shattuck's study for brandy and cigars, Larsen lingered at the table with Marie. He said, "I am an oldt man. The gompany of a young lady is more inspiring dan brandy. I stay."

Marie was suddenly frightened. Was he going to pry? To ask questions? Hurriedly, she said, "Sheriff, everybody says you are Swedish, but you do not sound like a Swede."

He chuckled. "My papa is Swedish, my mother was Flemish, undt I was born in Holland. I talk Swedish, Dutch, Flemish . . . undt some French.

"Mostly," he added, "I listen. I was listening to the druggist. He likes to talk, that one."

Though Marie was frightened, her expression did not change. She would not, she could not give them away. The strange rider had trusted her, and he had helped her. Perhaps nothing would have happened—not really—but no one had ever laid a hand on her before. Not in that way.

She must be careful, very careful. "I was in there tonight," she said calmly, "but I am afraid I gave him very little chance to talk."

His eyes twinkled. "A sheriff," he said, "in such a place as dis has to be more dan a sheriff. He must be chudge also. The courts," he added, "dey are far away. It is better we settle our own pusiness here."

She filled his cup, waiting for what had to come. When it did come she was surprised. He said, "A young girl . . . she must be careful. I do nodt ask what you do with the bandages."

She sat down suddenly opposite him. "I gave them to a man whom I believe to be an outlaw. I do not know that he is, and I do not care. Had it not been for him, I—"

She hesitated, and then without naming location or place, she described briefly what had happened.

"Ah, so? Strat should be more wise."

There was no need to ask questions. He fully understood the situation now, or believed that he did. But he was positive that the wounded outlaw would be one of the Colburn outfit.

What he had said was true. Court was a good long way off to the north; to get a prisoner there for trial was not difficult, but to get witnesses and a substantial case was extremely difficult. To be a sheriff called for a nicety of judgment, and also for sharpness of eye on one hand, blindness on the other. Some things had a way of straightening themselves out, and sometimes the removal of one factor in a situation caused things to settle down. Ed Larsen rarely made arrests, even more rarely did he go to court with one of those cases.

The Colburn gang were outlaws and wanted men, yet as outlaws went they were a decent lot. Bold, daring, and extremely shrewd, yes. But decent enough in their way. So far they had committed no crimes in his area; if cornered, he knew they would put up a desperate fight.

As he sat over his coffee he chuckled to himself. Marie had left the room, and now he sat alone, remembering the way she had carefully avoided mentioning any particular creek or place, and had avoided describing the outlaw. But trouble was coming, and he could not see his way clear to avoid it.

Only Dan Shattuck's seeming lack of interest had kept the pot from boiling over. Eustis, he knew, was fighting to get control, to take the lead that Shattuck had automatically enjoyed all these years.

Marie, it was obvious, had not told her uncle about Strat Spooner stopping her, for if she had, Dan would be riding to town with Pico and his hands right now, and within the hour Spooner would be strung to the nearest tree.

Ed Larsen put down his cup. It was up to him. He was going to have to see Spooner and order him to leave town.

He was, he felt, a reasonably brave man, but when he thought of Spooner something turned over inside him. Larsen had never been a gunfighter. He had fought Indians, hunted buffalo, and long ago had served a hitch in the army in Europe; but he was no match for Spooner with a pistol. Yet tell him he must.

McCarty was waiting for him when he left the dining room. "Riding in? Figured you might want company."

"I do," Larsen said. "I surely do."

Sampson McCarty was a man he could talk to, and he talked now as they rode away. He told him briefly and concisely the events of the day, even mentioning that he suspected the outlaw who had come to Marie's aid was one of the Colburn gang. Then he went on to speak of the bandages and medicines.

"It figures."

They rode on in silence for a while. Then McCarty spoke. "Ed, did you ever hear those rumors about there being five men in the Colburn outfit instead of the four everybody talks about?"

"Heard dem."

"There's only four now, anyway. There were only four at Casner Station."

"I t'ink you speak of dat other man in your paper one time."

McCarty dismissed the suggestion with a gesture. "I must have been mistaken. Nobody ever saw more than four that they could be sure of."

They rode on toward Rimrock, unaware that hands were being dealt in Rimrock that would alter the situation, and quickly.

Strat Spooner, left alone in the dark, splashed around in the water, trying to find his pistol. When he failed, he started in the direction his horse had gone; and in that, at least, he was lucky.

Not a quarter of a mile down the trail he found the horse, the bridle reins entangled in brush. He mounted and rode to Rimrock. By the time he arrived he was thoroughly chilled and in a murderous fury.

Nick Valentz was lying on his cot, reading a paper, and he turned his head to stare at Spooner, when he came in, still soaked to the hide.

"What the hell happened to you?"

"Shut up!"

Nick Valentz took another quick look at Spooner's eyes and remained silent. He watched the big gunman strip, dry himself with a dirty towel, and then dress once more.

Suddenly Spooner turned to him. "Heard you tell Hardcastle you'd seen Riley somewhere before—have you remembered where it was?"

Valentz hesitated. In this mood Spooner was dangerous, and he had no desire to provoke him, but he had promised Hardcastle, and that was where the money was.

"No," he said.

Spooner turned on him. "Damn you, Nick, if I find out you lied, I'll shove a shotgun barrel down your throat and let you have both barrels."

He would do it, too. Nick sat up slowly, touching his tongue to his lips. What was money, after all? He'd never seen a dead man spending it.

"I got an idea," he said, "only I ain't sure."

"Let's have it."

"I seen that Riley—I think it was him—over to Prescott one time. He was with Jim Colburn."

Spooner stamped his boot on the floor to settle his foot in it, and nodded with satisfaction. "Good! Damned good! Then that feller out to the creek was Kehoe."

"What are you talkin' about?"

"How much reward money would you say was ridin' on the Colburn gang?"

"Eight, maybe nine or ten thousand. Most of the money is on Weaver, but there are rewards out for all of them."

"Get on your feet. We're goin' over to see the boss. Then we're goin' to round up the boys and collect ourselves some fresh money. I know where that gang is at."

Martin Hardcastle sat alone in his office after Spooner and Valentz had gone. He had waited longer than he had planned, but the situation was now ripe. True, it had not gone just as he planned, with a cattle war over rustling between Shattuck and Riley, in the course of which Shattuck would be killed. Shattuck had for some unknown reason failed to react as expected, but this new situation was even better.

Strat Spooner would take his boys, with a few of the locals like that hot-headed Eustis thrown in, and they would strike at Riley's ranch in the Sweet Alice Hills. The Colburn gang would strike back and there would be shooting, and with known bandits in the country they would be blamed for whatever happened. The opportunity for which he had waited had come.

Hardcastle got to his feet and went to the back door of the saloon. Chata, a half-witted Mexican boy who slept in the shed back of the saloon, sometimes ran errands for him, and Hardcastle wanted him to go on one now. He gave him a dollar and a message for Dan Shattuck.

Then he returned to his room behind the bar and took a rifle from its case. He cleaned it carefully, then loaded it. He checked his six-gun with care, and reloaded it. This was one job he was going to do himself. He wouldn't miss it for anything.

"And after that," he said aloud, "Marie."

THIRTEEN

Gaylord Riley topped out of Fable Canyon and drew up on the rim of Dark Canyon Plateau. He was hot and tired, but the sun was going down and he had completed the job he had been planning.

He had cut out some of the best young breeding stock and herded them, with a young bull, into the lower part of Fable Valley where the grass was rich and they would be unlikely to stray.

Unknown to him, it was at this moment that Strat Spooner turned into the trail that was to take him to his meeting with Marie. Jim Colburn had already reached the ranch and was waiting to speak to Riley on his return.

Left alone in the canyon camp with Weaver, Parrish paced the ground and swore. He was no fool; he knew more about wounds than the others did, and he knew Weaver was in dire straits. Kept here, without medical attention, he would surely die. Drastic measures were needed, and Parrish decided suddenly that he would not wait for Colburn's return.

Swiftly, while Weaver muttered and cried out in his delirium, Parrish broke camp and packed up. What he was about to do might kill Weaver, but he would die here anyway. When he was packed and had the horses saddled, he went to Weaver. "We're pullin' out, Weaver," he said. "You got to get up."

Weaver had been an outlaw too long for the words not to reach him. If they were pulling out, there was danger and pulling out was necessary. With the help of Parrish he struggled to his feet and was helped into the saddle, where Parrish tied him.

Taking no time to destroy evidence of their camp, Parrish started out, leading Weaver's horse and the two pack horses. Colburn had been gone scarcely an hour, Kehoe even less.

All over the desert the strings were drawing tighter; men and events moved steadily toward a climax of which none of them were aware.

Riley rode into the ranch yard with the sun behind him, and the first person he saw was Colburn. The white-haired outlaw was walking toward him, and Cruz was standing in the door, watching.

Scarcely had Colburn begun to ask for help for Weaver, when Parrish, leading the horses, rode into camp. "Jim," he said, "I'm sorry. I couldn't wait."

"Cruz!" Riley yelled. "Fix a bed for him up at the house!"

While the Mexican worked swiftly to prepare a bed, Colburn and Riley untied Weaver and helped him from the saddle and into the house.

Gaylord Riley took one look at the wound and turned to the door, catching up his hat. "Where you off to?" Colburn asked.

"He needs a doctor, and there's one in Rimrock."

He waited for no argument, but went outside, shifted his saddle to a fresh horse, and turned into the trail to Rimrock. It was a long ride and a hard ride, but the dun he was riding was a stayer, and fast along with it.

McCarty was sitting on his bed with one boot off when he heard the pounding on the door. It was Riley.

"McCarty, you know Doc Beaman. We need him out at the ranch."

McCarty hesitated. "Beaman's got it in for you, Riley. He thinks you killed his nephew and stole his cattle."

"I can show him a bill of sale, but it makes no difference what he thinks of me. He's a doctor, and there's a man who needs help at the ranch. I'll have to take my chances."

Beaman was seated at his desk going over some accounts when McCarty and Riley came. He glanced at Riley, his face hardening.

"I hear you've no use for me," Riley said abruptly, "but that's neither here nor there. One of my hands has been shot, and he needs help the worst way."

"You're a damned murdering coyote," Beaman said coldly.

"Doc, if you say that to me after tonight you'd better have a gun in your hand. Tonight I need you too bad to resent anything you say. However, I've a witnessed bill of sale for those cattle."

"Witnessed?"

"Yes."

"That doesn't matter now." Doc Beaman got to his feet. "I'll see your man. After that we'll straighten this out once and for all, and don't think your talk of gun play intimidates me. I was using a gun before you were dry behind the ears."

When they arrived at the ranch Doc Beaman wasted no time. He glanced sharply at Kehoe, who stood outside; then he went into the house. He checked the wounded man's pulse, and unbound the wound.

He turned to Riley. "Did you get the bullet out?"

"No, I wasn't there. It's still inside him somewhere."

"It's got to come out, and no time wasted."

Suddenly there was a pound of a horse's hoofs in the yard, and Riley went swiftly to the door. Jim Colburn was at the bunkhouse door, Kehoe near the stable. Both held rifles.

It was Marie.

"Gaylord"—she called him by his first name for the first time—"you're going to be raided. Eustis and Strat Spooner

stopped by the ranch to get Uncle Dan. He would have no part
of it."

It was Riley who took charge now, and did so without
thinking. "Kehoe," he said quickly, "get up on the mountain.
There's a trail—you'll find it just past the corral over there.
You can see all over the country. When you see them, come on
down."

Doc Beaman had come to the door. "Marie, you can help
me. Come in here, will you?"

He turned back inside, and Riley followed. From a niche in
the wall he took a leather wallet and from it the bill of sale.

"Isn't that your nephew's signature? And there's the witness.
He's a bartender in Spanish Fork."

Beaman glanced at it. "Yes, that's Coker's hand. And I know
the bartender."

He pushed by. "No time for that now."

"I figured you ought to know . . . we're going to be attacked."

Beaman turned around sharply. "Damn it, man, I'm busy!
Keep them off me, that's all I ask! Keep them off if you want
this man to live!"

Riley went outside to Colburn and Parrish. "You heard him.
It's up to us."

"And to me, *amigo*," Cruz said. "I am one of you, am I not?"

"When this is over," Colburn said, "we'll ride out of here."

"If you do," Riley replied, "I go with you."

"What's that mean?" Colburn demanded.

"It means you're not leaving. Look, Jim. Weaver's fighting
for his life in there, and lucky to have the chance. Parrish had a
narrow escape just a while back. The odds are all against you,
and if you ride out of here you're riding into trouble, and you
all know it."

"So, then?"

"I need help, and you boys own part of this layout. My suggestion is you all stay on and work with me. You've got a
first-class Morgan stallion there, and we've got some mares.
This is good horse country. What I mean is, you boys have
ridden your last trail. You stay here, where you belong."

"And what about that Swede sheriff?"

"I've got a hunch he knows who I am, and he's left me alone. He made a remark once about giving things a chance, and I believe he meant me. Well, I think he'll give you a chance, too."

Jim Colburn stared out over the hills. He would be a fool not to admit that he was tired—tired of running, tired of being on the dodge. It would be good to settle down, to have friends, to smell the smoke of branding fires and handle a rope again.

"I think he's right, Jim," Parrish said, "and I can speak for Kehoe. We've been talking about quitting. The fact is, Kehoe would have quit a long time ago but for you—he didn't want to leave you holding the bag."

Colburn continued to gaze at the hills. He had gotten into this business without really intending to, and there never had seemed a way out. Now there was. He had taken money with a gun, now he could repay it in a measure by building something.

He paused to ask himself whether he really meant it, or whether the old night trails would call again; but no sooner had he put the question to himself than he knew all the desire had gone out of him. They had been wild young cowboys when they began; now they were men, and it was time to change. It was just lucky that they had been given the chance.

It was a strange thing that the boy they had tried to save was now to save them all.

"All right, Riley," Colburn said, "we're workin' for you."

Strat Spooner drew up where Trail Canyon cut off on the left. "There's no way out of that hole," he said, indicating Trail Canyon, "but Nick, you take four men and go around through Ruin Canyon and come across the saddle and take them from the north. We'll hold on here, and when we move in we'll go in fast an' shootin'—hit anybody who ain't on a horse."

"How many will there be?" Nick Valentz asked.

"Four—maybe five. One man is down sick, and likely the rest will be scattered."

"There's Riley, Cruz, and Lewis. You forgettin' them?"

"There's eighteen of us," Spooner said. "As for Darby Lewis, he'll cut an' run. Anyway, he's over in the basin, an' there's scarcely a chance he'll show up."

"All right," Valentz agreed, "but when do we go in?"

"Right at daylight. You get in position, and when I shoot, you come a-foggin' it."

Spooner and the others stayed there, and nobody talked for a while. They dismounted and huddled about, smoking and shielding the glow of their cigarettes in cupped palms. Nick Valentz and his men had swung down Ruin Canyon toward the basin, and it would take time for them to get into position.

Spooner's waiting place was almost a mile and a half from Kehoe's place up on the Sweet Alice Hills. Once, Kehoe thought he heard a distant sound, but it was not repeated and it could have been a falling rock or some small animal scurrying around in the darkness.

But Kehoe was restless. The knowledge that an attack might come and leave him marooned on top of the mountain worried him, and after a time he decided to slip down closer to the trail.

For a while there had been lights and movement down at the ranch, which was plainly in view, nearly five hundred feet lower down and due west. He went to his horse and mounted.

Marie appeared at the door of the house. "Gaylord, can I get some fresh water?" she asked. "Doc wants to boil his instruments."

Cruz came out of the shadows and took the bucket, and walked away toward the spring.

Marie stood beside Riley in the darkness. "How does he look?" Riley whispered.

"Bad . . . very bad. Doc is really worried."

Neither spoke for a minute and then Marie said, "Gaylord, was this the reason you wouldn't say anything the other night? Because these men were your friends?"

"Do you know who they are?"

"Kehoe told me."

"Yes, they are my friends. I was one of them."

"But you quit."

"Yes . . . and they put up part of the money to give me my chance. You see how it is."

"Did you think it would make a difference to me? You know it wouldn't."

The night was very still. The stars hung low. It was almost morning, although there was still no hint of gray in the sky. But here it became light very quickly, for they were high up.

Gaylord Riley stared at the stars, aware of the girl by his side, but thinking rather of what this night meant to him, to them both. This was an out-and-out attack, and partly by the townspeople and ranchers, even if the bulk of the attackers would be the hired gunmen who had been holed up over near the Blues.

Some of those who got hurt might be ranchers like Eustis or Bigelow, but once the battle opened nothing could be done about that. They would be shooting, and they would be shot at, perhaps killed.

No matter what happened, he intended to stay, and to keep the others with him. Somewhere, sometime a man had to take a stand, and this was his stand. Besides, he now had something worth fighting for.

At least, Dan Shattuck had refused to join them. That much was favorable.

Cruz returned with the water, and Marie followed him into the house, leaving Riley alone.

His fingers went to the fully loaded cartridge belt around his hips, then to the bandolier of cartridges across his chest. He walked toward the trail entrance, listening.

There was no sound.

Dan Shattuck rode reluctantly westward with the note in his pocket. The handwriting was strange to him, for he had never had occasion to see anything written by Martin Hardcastle. The message was plain and right to the point, and the note unsigned.

If you want evidence, ten head of your steers are penned up near the ruins at House Park Butte. They are fresh branded to 5B.

There were several ways in which a Lazy S could be changed into a 5B, which was Gaylord Riley's brand. Eager as he was to apprehend whoever had been rustling his cattle, Shattuck feared to discover that Riley was actually the one.

So he had said nothing to anyone on receiving the note, which had been thrust under his door, but had saddled up and ridden away in the night. If he could come upon the cattle at House Park Butte he might find evidence that would convince him. And if such evidence was found, he would join the attackers.

House Park Butte was a towering rock mass that almost divided the basin where Riley was reported to be running his cattle, and it was only a few miles north of the ranch on Dark Canyon Plateau.

Shattuck had a good horse, and he rode swiftly. No longer a young man, he was wiry and strong, and had been born to the saddle. Furthermore, he knew the country over which he must ride. Skirting Salt Creek Mesa, he followed a dim trail toward the butte.

Martin Hardcastle, who knew most things that went on, did not know that Chata, the Mexican boy, had a hero. Chata lived in abject fear of Hardcastle, and obeyed his every command, and in return Hardcastle saw that he was fed and occasionally gave him money; but all that meant nothing, compared to his idol.

That idol was a man of his own people. He was a top hand, a skilled hand with a rope, a fine horseman, and an excellent shot. That idol was Pico, and, being so close, Chata could not resist the chance to look upon him once more.

At the Lazy S bunkhouse Chata crept stealthily to the door. There he paused, fearful of going further. From within came the sound of snores, and the door stood open, for the night was cool though far from cold. He edged nearer, wanting at least a glimpse of his hero, and perhaps a glimpse of the gun he carried.

"Chata"—the voice was low but Chata jumped as if struck—"what are you doing here?"

Pico was seated on the edge of his bunk, a pistol in his hand.

"It was only to look," Chata said, "to see the *pistola.*"

"You've seen it. Now you'd better go. You might be shot, prowling around like that."

He spoke in a low tone and in Spanish. As he finished he suddenly realized the boy's presence on the ranch could scarcely be accidental.

"Chata, tell me, what are you doing out here? Why did you come?"

Chata hesitated. It was a rule of Señor Hardcastle that one did not speak of the messages carried, or the errands done. Until now he had obeyed that rule, but now—*this was Pico!*

"It was a message for Señor Shattuck."

What message? He did not know, only it had come from Señor Hardcastle . . . only he was not to say that.

Had he given the message to Shattuck? No, he had pushed it under the door, and then had hidden when Shattuck came to look.

What did the message say? Chata replied that he could not read English. Of course, he could read the brand—brands were the same in any language, he thought.

What brand? The 5B. There were also some letters, large letters as in brands, but these were the beginnings of words. They were H—, P—, B—, and the words were not long words.

Pico was thoroughly alarmed. He knew now the sound that had awakened him had been that of a horse. Chata's pony, or a horse ridden by Dan Shattuck? All he really knew was that

Dan Shattuck had gone off into the night, directed by an unsigned message, and undoubtedly riding into a trap.

He dressed swiftly and went to the house. Dan Shattuck's bed was empty, the office was empty. He had taken his gun belt and Winchester.

As Pico slapped a saddle on a horse, he considered the names of places. Undoubtedly the 5B restricted the area somewhat, for only two things would have gotten Dan Shattuck into a saddle in the middle of the night. Rustling, or something to do with Marie.

The 5B was Riley's brand, and Riley had been accused of rustling, therefore Pico headed out for the 5B, riding fast. As he rode, he ran over in his mind all the place names he could think of that had some relation to the 5B area.

Maverick Point . . . the Seven Sisters . . . Mormon Pasture . . . Salt Creek Mesa . . . Bridger Jack . . . Big Pocket . . . Deadman Point . . . Dark Canyon . . . Cathedral Butte . . . Butte—that B might stand for Butte.

Gyp Canyon . . . the Basin . . . And then he had it: *House Park Butte!*

Pico had never been known to spur a horse. He spurred one now.

FOURTEEN

The night was alive with movement. There was a stirring in the canyons, a whisper of sound upon the mesa that was not of wind or coyote passing. Even the wild animals held still, ears pricked to the strange sounds.

Here a hoof touched stone, a saddle's leather creaked, or a spur jingled. Somewhere wiry brush scraped on a leather chap, a restless horse pawed, and a man cleared his throat. They were small sounds, but different sounds, and every animal ear was alert, for none knew which was the quarry, none could be sure where the pursuit would end.

The stars alone were still, and in the brooding darkness the rocks cast their deeper shadows.

Within the ranch house on Dark Canyon the man called Weaver had regained consciousness and was resting easily, the bullet gone from his body.

He looked up at Riley. "They shouldn't have done it, Lord. They shouldn't have brought me here."

"You belong here. This is your home."

In the dimly lit room Weaver's features were drawn and pale, and Riley felt the cold hand of fear run along his spine.

He, who had no family, knew these men were his family, these men from the outlaw trail, and he had taken them, for better or worse.

"Rest easy, man," he said quietly. "You've come home."

He turned then and stepped out into the darkness. Nobody spoke, no sound was made, yet he could feel the movement in the night. Canyons and deserts have their own small sounds, for even the lonely places are not still. They have their small movements, their restlessness, but tonight it was not the same. Nor was it merely that he was so keenly alert. He was not imagining things. He knew there was trouble out there, and that it momentarily drew nearer and nearer.

His ears had grown selective with wilderness living, and he knew each sound that was different. His ears tuned out the usual noises, or ignored them. It was the strange sounds that he heard, or the lack of sound, which was in itself a warning. When the insects stopped their singing it was because something was near, something not known, not understood.

He cradled his Winchester now in the hollow of his arm and looked toward the mountain where Kehoe was. No word from him—was that good or bad?

Dan Shattuck walked his horse up to the ruins near House Park Butte, and found they were deserted. He scouted them carefully, peering at the ground, striving to see what tracks, if any, were visible. Morning was near, and it was already light enough to see that there were no tracks but those of cattle since the rains, and these were wandering, grazing cattle, not driven by anyone.

He straightened up in the saddle, and suddenly he was afraid.

He had been a damned fool to ride all the way over here without help. He should at least have called Pico and told him. Pico would have wanted him to have company, and would have insisted on coming himself. Right now Shattuck was wishing Pico were here.

He looked around carefully. There was a corral, an old pole corral over near the spring just west of the butte. That might be where the stock was being held. He drew his Winchester from its scabbard, and worked his way cautiously through the junipers.

As he moved slowly toward the almost hidden corral, other events were moving toward a climax. He heard, suddenly, the sound of horses, and drew up sharply. Swinging down, he caught his horse's nose and held it tight against a whinny.

In the vague light, five riders swept by. Nick Valentz he recognized. The others were strangers—one of them a drifter he had once seen around Hardcastle's. When they had gone by, he went on.

At that very moment, a few miles to the south, Strat Spooner glanced down at his watch. It was almost time. Nick should be getting into position now.

A few miles to the westward of where Shattuck waited in the cedars to watch Valentz pass, Darby Lewis awakened to what was to be his last morning on earth.

It was faintly gray in the east, but he woke suddenly, sharply, as though startled by some sound, yet there was no sound. He clasped his hands behind his head and stared up at the stars. He had chosen to bed down in the basin rather than ride back to the ranch, but this morning he felt different about it. In the first place, he was through here for the time; and in the second place, he wanted some of that good coffee that Cruz always made.

Besides, he was due for some time in town. He had stayed on this job long enough, and he wanted to see the girls and have a few drinks; maybe a hand or two of poker.

He rolled out of bed, put on his hat and then his jeans. The more he thought of going to town, the more the idea pleased him. He dressed, rolled his bed, and strapped it behind the saddle. Mounting up, he started for the ranch. The trail he chose was a dim one up South Canyon. There would be quite a scramble when he reached the plateau, but he had used the short cut once before.

He crossed the saddle and was topping out on the plateau when he saw the riders. They were crossing the open country ahead of him while his approach was still masked by junipers.

He knew those riders, for he had on occasion rustled cattle with some of them. Nick Valentz he knew very well, and he had never liked him. The instant he saw them he guessed what was happening. The ranchers were attacking Riley, and Nick Valentz somehow was in on it.

He knew a sneak attack when he saw one, and he knew this must be only a small part of the movement. At the ranch they were probably asleep, and so far as he knew, Riley and Cruz were alone there.

He had his chance now. He was out of the fight. He was off to one side, and nobody was expecting him back right now. He could go back and hole up in one of the canyons north of the basin and wait until it was all over. After all, he had been planning to draw his time.

He could get away all right. He could go back the way he'd come; he could cut and run down the length of Wild Cow Point, or he could let the riders pass and then back-trail the attackers into Rimrock.

He did none of those things. For suddenly, and almost with relief, Darby Lewis knew the time had come to make a stand.

It was a strange decision, for all his life he had been a drifter with the currents, letting them carry him where they would. Now he had his chance to get out and stay out, and suddenly he knew he was not going to do it.

He drew his Winchester, lifted it, and squeezed off a shot. He had never shot a man in the back and did not wish to now. It might have been that which spoiled his aim, for he missed a shot that should have been a clean hit.

Valentz turned sharply in his saddle, his face a mask of startled fear and fury. He lifted his rifle and Darby Lewis fired again, and that time he did not miss. The bullet caught Valentz in the chest and tore through him, tearing his heart open as it passed.

Darby Lewis, knowing he must warn those at the ranch,

raced for the shelter of some boulders, firing as he rode. All four of the riders had turned their guns on him, and he felt the smash of their bullets. There was no pain, just three solid blows, two almost simultaneous, the last an instant later. Darby felt himself falling, but managed to cling for an instant to the pommel before letting go. He hit the ground on his back and rolled over.

With a shock he realized he had caught it good, but he levered a shell into his rifle and, as the first man charged into the rocks after him, Darby Lewis fired the rifle into his chest, even as the bullets smashed him back into the grass.

Darby Lewis rolled to his side, felt the wetness of blood against his skin, and he stared at the dead man, blinking slowly. His lids seemed very heavy.

He recognized the man as one of the gunmen he had seen around Hardcastle's, and he chuckled. He had never counted himself a gunhand, just a cowboy working for wages, but here in a few seconds he had ticked off Nick Valentz and this one.

Using the butt of his rifle, he pulled himself along the ground by digging it into the earth. He got himself out into the sun, and said aloud, "I don't want to die in the dark."

It was the last thing he ever said, and it would take the circling buzzards, hours later, to tell the survivors at the ranch that Darby Lewis had gone out shooting.

At the sound of the shots, Strat Spooner swore viciously and slammed the spurs into the flanks of his horse. When they reached the ranch their horses were at a dead run, and they broke into the open, fanning out swiftly.

Confident of their numbers, they had taken no time to scout the area. What they charged was not the half-built encampment to be found on most new ranches, but a solidly built log house, a bunkhouse of logs, and a stable with a nearly flat roof and a parapet around it, equipped with loopholes.

Jim Colburn heard them coming. "There," he said to Parrish. "You take them on the left, I'll take the right."

The first man who came into the open ground was yelling

like a Comanche, but the yells choked off, for Colburn's bullet had smashed through his throat and chin.

The man plunged forward, falling under the feet of the horses that followed. In the pile-up that lasted for seconds only, Parrish smashed a rider from the saddle, and then both men fired again.

Riley, crouched on top of the stable, had not fired at all, knowing the longer he could keep his position concealed, the better.

The surprise planned by Spooner had failed, and there would be no more charges. From now on the fight would be tougher, with moving and sniping, seeking out targets, and every shot a risk.

Riley kept down and studied the terrain about him. Twice he saw moving men, but he held his fire. He chose three possible targets, drew a bead on the place where each was likely to appear, and made three dry runs, swinging his rifle to cover each of the three spots.

A gun thundered and glass crashed at the house. Riley swore—it had been hell, packing that glass in here. Then came a volley, with all shots concentrated on the house.

Suddenly the men below started to move. One of Riley's selected targets was a man in a checked shirt, and as the man lifted from his crouching position among the trees to lunge forward, Riley shot him, instantly swinging to targets two and three. His shot at target two was wasted, for there was nothing there; at three, a man dove for shelter, yelping with surprise.

They would be ready for him now, so he abandoned the roof, dropping through the trap door into the hay. As he landed in the hay, a man standing just inside the barn door whirled about to stare up at him in shocked surprise. Riley was off balance, but he fired from the hip, and the man dropped quickly, firing in return. Both men missed. Instantly, both fired again, and Riley hit the hay rolling over.

When he rolled up to his knees to fire again, the man was gone. He had darted down the slope from the door, and outside a gun roared . . . then came a second shot.

Kehoe appeared suddenly in the doorway. "Got him," he said.

Outside there was sudden and complete silence. Among the attackers there were tough, gun-hardened men, veterans of cattle wars and outlawry, but there were saddle tramps, too, drifters who had joined up for fighting wages, and who now were getting more fighting than they had bargained for. A rushing, surprise attack on a few men taken unawares was one thing. To attack half a dozen entrenched men, battle-hardened and ready, was quite another.

Suddenly there was a sound of a retreating horse, in full flight—somebody had had enough. The contagion spread, and another man left, then another. This last one was Eustis.

Two bullets had seemed to come near him . . . actually they had been some distance off; but the sound of a ricochet can often be heard by several people in completely opposite directions and each will swear the bullet had passed close—a near miss.

There are few more unpleasant sounds than a ricocheting bullet, and Eustis's pugnacity evaporated. All at once it came home to him that he himself might be killed—that hanging rustlers, no matter how guilty or otherwise, might prove to be dangerous work.

His ranch was some distance off and if he was going to make it in time for lunch, he would have to hurry. He made it in time, but he had no appetite.

There were a few sporadic, defiant shots, but the attack was over.

Gus Enloe, his calfskin vest still intact, led the shattered remnants back to Rimrock. Of those who had ventured the raid, seven were dead, and several more had wounds. Strat Spooner was not among them.

Strat was a man who used his gun for hire, and he had no intention of getting killed. He was the second man through the gap when the first rush took place, and when he had swept on through he turned once to look back. Two of his men were down, and he had no taste for that sort of shooting. Besides, he

had other things on his mind. As he rode through he had
noticed a saddled horse at the corral . . . it was Marie Shattuck's
mare.

Sooner or later Marie would be going home.

Gaylord Riley walked slowly back across the ranch yard in
the sunlight of the early morning. Off to the west the upper
walls of the vast red canyons were bright with the risen sun;
shadows still lay beyond the mountains to the east, and darkness held in the canyon depths. He stood for a moment in the
ranch yard, looking off toward the east, where the riders had
fled, circling the ranch, taking any way they could to escape.

Marie came out from the house. "Are you all right?"

"We were lucky," he said, "all of us."

"I am going back with Sampson McCarty," she said. "Doc
will stay on a little longer."

"Thanks for bringing him."

They stood together, enjoying the warmth, their minds empty
of thought, half numbed by the shock of events. They simply
absorbed the warmth, the clear air, the faint smell of woodsmoke
from the house fire.

"When this is all over," Riley said, "I'll be riding to call."

"Do that," she said.

In the sickroom Weaver lay alone, listening to the stillness.
He could hear the faint murmur of voices, but there was no
other sound. Cruz and Kehoe had gone from the room, but the
faint, acrid smell of gunpowder remained. It was an old smell,
a familiar smell.

He lay very quiet, completely comfortable, wanting nothing
at all.

The wild, hard-riding days were over now, and the boys
were settled. He had been right about the kid, right all along.
Maybe when his own sins were totaled and his failures accounted,
this would add up to something on his side of the ledger.
Weaver rolled himself up on one elbow and looked out the
window, the glass shattered by rifle shots.

The air was cool. It felt good and carried the smell of the pines. At this moment Weaver knew that he was going to die.

He had been feeling better. He had enjoyed the sound of the guns. He had lived to that sound, and he would die by it.

There was something yet to be done. He pulled over a piece of brown wrapping paper that lay on the table and wrote painfully:

Last Will and Tesimint of Ira Weaver. Everything to the kid, Gaylord Riley. Hang up your spurs Jim, Parry, and Kehoe. I'm lightin a shuck.

Ira Weaver

He lay back on the bed and looked up at the ceiling. He could hear the voices of the kid and his girl out there, a low murmur.

"Well, I'll be damned!" he said aloud, and he smiled as he said it. "I got my boots off!" Slightly amazed and quite pleased, he died.

FIFTEEN

For a long time after Valentz and those who accompanied him had passed, Shattuck remained where he was. Uneasily, he had the feeling he should pull out and return to the ranch. There were things happening here in which he had wanted no part, and he had come this morning hoping more to have the note disproved than proved.

Marie was in love with Gaylord Riley—that he believed. If Riley was actually a rustler, he feared to know it for the truth for her sake. She had been his only family for many years, his only excuse for being.

He had been irritated by Riley's purchase of white-face cattle. He had faced that issue and admitted it, reluctantly, to himself. He had enjoyed a childish pride in being the only owner of white-face cattle, and it was that pride even more than fear of rustling that had been hurt.

He had not for a minute believed anyone could bring that herd of cattle down from Spanish Fork, but it seemed beyond doubt that Riley had done it. Which meant that he knew of some trail other than those usually traveled.

The Outlaw Trail, to be widely known in later years, was at

this time no more than a rumor. The few who had ridden across the San Rafael Swell had spoken of lack of water—scarcely enough water for even a small party, let alone a herd of cattle. Nevertheless, the Mormons who had gone into the San Juan country had crossed that country somewhere. His knowledge of their trek was vague, but he knew it had been accomplished.

The fact remained that Riley had brought his cattle down across the country, and had become one of the largest ranchers in the area by that one trip. Which indicated he was a man of enterprise, perhaps a man of vision.

Dan Shattuck took a cigar from his vest pocket and clipped the tip, then put the cigar between his teeth. He knew he should ride out of here, and now.

It was at that moment that he heard the shooting that led to the death of Darby Lewis and two others. The shots were distant, but clear enough. He listened to them, started to turn his horse, and then hesitated.

He must know. Marie must never marry a thief, a rustler. He rode forward toward the old corral. And it was empty.

The sun that was to rise upon battle at Riley's ranch, that was to shine upon death along Dark Canyon Plateau, had not yet risen. The morning was gray with the light that precedes the sun, but it was light enough to see that not only was the old corral empty, but that it showed no evidence of being used in many months.

Beyond the corral there was a slight slope, covered with aspen. Some small movement drew his eyes to that slope as Martin Hardcastle stepped from among the trees, holding a Winchester.

"You turned me off, Shattuck," he said hoarsely. "You made light of me. You held me as unfit to marry your niece."

Dan Shattuck looked into Hardcastle's eyes with a fine contempt. "Of course, Hardcastle," he said quietly. "Of course. My niece has a mind of her own, and she will marry whoever she wishes, but certainly not you. You've run a saloon, you've trafficked in women. You're no fit man for any decent girl. You should have known better than to ask."

"I'll have her," Hardcastle said, "one way or another. Without you, there ain't nobody to stand in my way, and you'll be dead."

Shattuck measured the time in his mind. How far could he draw a gun before the bullet struck him? He had never been a fast man with a gun . . . he would have to be now.

"You're mistaken." He watched, hoping the gun muzzle would dip or sway to give him an added chance. "My niece is in love with young Riley. If you weren't so blindly concerned with yourself you'd have seen that."

"Riley?" Hardcastle was astonished. "That kid? You're crazy!"

Shattuck shrugged ever so slightly, and managed to move his hand an inch closer to the gun butt. "She told me so herself," he lied, "and she's up there at the ranch with him now."

"She'll be killed! There's going to be a raid on the ranch!"

Shattuck said nothing, but inched his hand back a bit farther. His mouth was dry, but his eyes never wavered from Hardcastle.

"I'll have her," Hardcastle said again. "Strat will kill Riley, and I'll have her."

"You'll have to kill Ed Larsen and Sampson McCarty too," Shattuck said. "They'll not allow such a thing to happen."

"Like hell! I—"

Dan Shattuck made his try. His hand swept back, grasping the gun butt, but even as his fingers closed around the butt he felt the shock of the bullet, and fell with the whip of another one near his skull. He hit the ground and lay still, not quite unconscious.

Hardcastle walked to his horse and stepped into the saddle, glancing at the still figure that lay upon the ground, and at the dark stain of the blood.

"If you aren't dead yet," he said, "you soon will be."

He reined his horse around, holding the rifle ready, but there was no stirring of the muscles, no flicker of movement. He half lifted the rifle for another shot, but why? The man was dead.

He stared at the body, feeling the stirring of triumph. The damned old fool—to try to stand in the way of Martin Hardcastle!

He heard the sound of the running horse, and turned in shocked surprise. Even before he saw the horse itself, he caught a glimpse of the Mexican sombrero.

Pico!

He had forgotten Pico.

He jacked a shell into the chamber and lifted the rifle, ready for a quick shot.

Pico swept into the open at a dead run. Hardcastle's rifle leaped up and he fired—a wide miss. He swung his horse, lifted the rifle again, and saw Pico charging at him.

He was no such rider as the vaquero, no such shot. He fired, but not quickly enough. The Mexican was riding right at him and suddenly, when not ten feet separated them, Pico's pistol began to blossom with crimson blasts of fire.

Hardcastle never even got another cartridge into the chamber, for the Mexican was too close. Holding his pistol low, Pico triggered the gun three times into Hardcastle's belly.

Martin Hardcastle felt the solid blows, trip-hammer blows in the belly, and he felt himself falling. He grabbed wildly at the pommel, but his horse was racing away, burned by one of the bullets. Hardcastle's shoulders hit the ground, his foot still caught in the stirrup.

The plunging horse raced through a patch of dead brush, Hardcastle's body bounding alongside. On through a patch of small rocks, over a stretch of lava. For a quarter of a mile Hardcastle's heavy body bounced and smashed against brush and rocks, and then his boot pulled off, releasing his foot. Even now he was still conscious, still aware.

The horse's hoofs clattered upon rocks, pounded upon earth, and then it was gone.

Martin Hardcastle lay torn and bleeding, his body raw and lacerated, and in his belly the holes of three bullets, one of which had gone on to nick his spine.

An hour later, unable to move, his body one vast ocean of pain, he saw the first buzzard in the sky. It swung in a wide, lazy circle.

And then there were two.

SIXTEEN

Gaylord Riley looked around, taking stock. So much had happened in so short a time. There were the bodies of two men to be moved; undoubtedly others lay out in the brush.

The others emerged, and Cruz walked toward the house. Doc Beaman checked the bodies of the fallen men, then followed Cruz inside. Nobody said anything, nobody felt like talking. Tell Sackett, who was leaving, went to the corral to catch up his horse. Marie had gone. She had ridden off with McCarty.

Colburn and Parrish went out to where Nick Valentz lay. "Knew him down on the Brazos, years ago," Parrish commented. "Never was any good. Spooner an' him, they've run together for years."

They had begun to dig graves when they heard the sound of horses. Riley came out, easing his pistol in its holster.

It was Pico, and seated on another horse was Dan Shattuck. "The doctor is here? He is hurt . . . bad."

They got Shattuck inside, and Doc Beaman got busy again. For a while it was touch and go; but Beaman was a good doctor, and Shattuck was a strong man. After a time the doctor came out with a satisfied look on his face. "He'll live," he said.

Riley stood beside the corral while Sackett saddled his horse. "If you're this way again, stop by."

Sackett accepted his wages. "I might be," he said. "I'm a drifting man."

It was mid-morning before Ed Larsen rode into the ranch yard. He turned in his saddle, looking around. There was little to see. The bodies had been taken to their gravesides, the patches of blood covered with fresh sand.

Riley went out to meet him and, as carefully as possible, explained what had happened. Doc Beaman stood beside him, listening. At last he said, "That's the way it was, Ed. They were attacked and they defended themselves."

When Larsen had ridden on toward the corrals, Doc Beaman said, "That man in there . . . he died."

Riley could only stare at him, for he had no words. Weaver dead . . . in a way he had expected it. That wound had gone too long without care. At least, he was out of it.

Sheriff Larsen glanced slowly around, then dismounted. "I could drink coffee," he said, and followed them into the house.

Holding a cup in his hands he glanced over at Colburn. "That last time I saw you I vorked in a store in Dodge. You rode for Pierce . . . came over the trail with him. You hadt the name of being of goot hand." He tasted his coffee, and glanced at Cruz with respect. "I chudge a man by his actions," he said.

When he was gone, Colburn looked after him, then smiled and said, "Riley, I never thought I'd really *like* a sheriff!"

Jim Colburn walked to the door with Riley. "All right, Lord," he said, at last, "we will stay . . . as long as we cause you no trouble."

"This will end it," Riley said.

"Then one last order from your old boss. Go see that girl, and don't waste time. Go now!"

Strat Spooner was a careful man and he knew the penalty for molesting a woman in western country. But the time for thinking reasonably was past, for he was a man obsessed.

Moreover, with the country in a turmoil over the raid on the 5B, with the drifters leaving the country in all directions, it would be difficult if not impossible to say which one of so many had done what he planned to do at the Shattuck ranch.

He took his time, keeping to low country and utilizing every bit of cover, for he did not wish to be seen at all. Yet he made no effort to cover his tracks until he rode on the range that was claimed by Dan Shattuck. Once, from the shoulder of Horse Mountain, he saw Marie. She was riding with someone in a black coat, which could only mean Sampson McCarty or the doctor. And the chances were they would ride on toward town when she turned off to follow the trail to the Lazy S.

He checked his guns again. There was little to worry about. At this time of year Shattuck usually had only two hands aside from Pico. They would be miles away, over on the Horsehead where Shattuck ran most of his cattle.

The old cook was sure to be there, but he would offer no opposition.

From a hilltop near the ranch, Strat Spooner sat and smoked, watching the place. He saw Marie arrive alone, saw the cook come to the door to throw out some water, but after an hour he had seen nobody else. At this time of day, if anyone was on the place they would surely be moving around. He got to his feet, brushing off his pants.

He would go down there like he was riding the grub line. Nobody in the West ever turned down a hungry man. Once inside, the rest would be easy, and he would know in a few minutes if anyone else was around.

He felt oddly excited, but nervous too. His mouth was dry and he kept wetting his lips. He turned several times to look all around, but he saw no one. He rode into the ranch yard at a walk, eyes alert for any movement.

He knew the favorite horses of both Dan Shattuck and Pico, and both were gone.

He tied his horse with a slip knot and went up to the kitchen door, which stood open. He thrust his head into the door. "How's for some coffee?"

He looked past the cook at the open door that led to the rest of the house. From inside he heard faint stirrings of sound.

Baldwin, who had cooked for Dan Shattuck ever since they left Baltimore together, was frightened. He knew Strat Spooner, and knew that, while any man might stop for a bite to eat, it was highly unlikely that Strat would stop, knowing how he was regarded on the Lazy S.

"Just in time," Baldwin said quietly. He filled a cup, and was surprised to see that his hand was trembling.

The old Negro was shrewd, and he realized that Spooner had not come here by accident. Moreover, he had arrived only a few minutes after Miss Marie had come in.

He placed a steaming cup of coffee on the table and a large slab of apple pie. He did not like Spooner, but the apple pie might put him in a pleasant mood, and might get him out of here. Mr. Shattuck and Pico had left hours ago . . . no telling when they would be back.

Strat Spooner sat down and picked up the coffee cup. His ears were alert to the slightest sound from the other part of the house, and he was sure only one person was there—at least, only one who moved about.

The kitchen was a spacious room; the adjoining room was the dining room where the crew ate, and Shattuck and his niece as well when they were not entertaining guests. Suddenly, he heard the sound of quick, light steps in the hall, and Marie came into the kitchen.

She stopped abruptly, chilled by fear. Strat Spooner, after what had happened upon the trail, would never dare come here unless certain she was alone.

"Howdy, ma'am," he said easily. "Glad to see you lookin' so well."

Fighting a desire to turn and run, she said "Ned, Uncle Dan will be back soon. You'd best prepare dinner for Pico too."

"That Riley feller had fighting friends," Spooner commented. "I never figured he was so much himself."

"Don't ever be foolish enough to try him," she replied coldly.

"Glad Shattuck and that Mexican ain't to home. That was the one thing had me puzzled."

Ned Baldwin regretted for the first time that he kept no gun in the kitchen. There never had been need for one, and he was not a man who liked guns, although he knew how to use one.

Marie turned as if to walk into the other part of the house, but Strat's voice stopped her. "Don't be in a hurry, Marie," he said. "I ain't through talking."

"I have nothing to say to you," she replied.

"Set down," he said, indicating the seat opposite him. "Might as well join me."

Baldwin cleared his throat. "You finish your coffee, Spooner," he said, "and get out of here."

A large butcher knife lay on the cutting board and he turned sharply toward it.

Without rising, Strat Spooner swung a backhand blow with the heavy white crockery cup and struck the old Negro on the temple. He dropped as if shot.

Marie ran to the old man, her face stricken. "You—you've killed him!"

"I doubt it." Spooner took out the makings and began to build a cigarette while he watched them.

Then reaching out swiftly, he caught her arm and jerked her to her feet, and thrust her into the hall that led to the living room. Spurs jingling, he pushed her ahead of him, then threw her from him to a divan.

"No use to make any fuss," he said, drawing on his cigarette. "It ain't going to do you a mite of good." He flicked the ash from his cigarette and grinned insolently. "An' you'd better hope nobody comes. I'd only have to kill them."

"Pico will be coming!"

"That Mex don't worry me none." He crossed the room and took a bottle of whiskey from the sideboard, and two glasses. He filled the glasses, put down the bottle, and handed a glass to her. "Here, have a drink. An' don't say I ain't generous."

"I don't drink."

Spooner was enjoying himself, but his eyes kept straying

toward the windows. He was not going to hurry this, nor was he going to be surprised.

"Have one anyway."

"No!"

The amused smile left his lips. "You take it, and you drink! Otherwise I'll force it down you."

She took the glass, then deliberately she threw the whiskey at his eyes; but he had been expecting some such move and struck her hand. She would not have believed a big man could move so swiftly. He knocked the glass from her hand, then slapped her with his open palm.

The blow brought her to her knees, but almost instantly she was on her feet, her head ringing with the force of the blow. Quickly, she put the table between them. Picking up the bottle he took another drink; then, smiling, he reached over to the table and pushed it slowly toward the wall. There was no place to go, and there was no weapon in the room.

And then they both heard a walking horse outside.

Spooner swore and, drawing his gun, stepped quickly to the side of a window. Then he laughed. A riderless horse stood in the yard, and it was Dan Shattuck's horse.

Pico, in taking Shattuck to the Riley ranch, had caught the nearest horse, which happened to be Hardcastle's. Left alone, Shattuck's horse had returned home.

Spooner turned back to the room. "Honey, you'd better be nice to Strat. Your uncle ain't comin' home. That was his horse, and there's blood on the saddle."

Unmindful of Spooner, she ran to the window and caught back the curtain. One rein was hung around the pommel, the other dragged on the ground. There *was* blood on the saddle, and some across the side of the horse.

A floor board creaked and she dodged away just in time, for Spooner was almost upon her. Swiftly she moved away, turning a chair into his path. He stopped for another drink, took it while watching her with an amused smile, and came on. . . .

*   *   *

Gaylord Riley had also seen the riderless horse, and recognized it. He slowed up, wondering what to tell Marie about her uncle. His horse was walking in from the woods, and not on the main trail, and an instant before he entered the yard he saw Strat Spooner's horse.

He remembered the horse clearly from the attack that morning, and Kehoe had told him about the scene he had interrupted at the creek.

In an instant he was on the ground and was walking swiftly toward the kitchen door, his eyes shifting from window to window. The door was closed, but easing it gently open, he saw the cook lying on the floor, his head bloody from a lacerated scalp.

From the living room he heard a man's low chuckle, and then a sudden scurry of movement. Tiptoeing to the door, he saw Spooner standing facing Marie, half turned toward him.

There was fear in Marie's eyes, the fear of a trapped animal. Seeing it, Riley felt something rise inside him, a feeling he had felt to that same degree since the night those men had killed his father.

"Hello, Strat," he said.

Marie gasped, and Strat's shoulders bunched as if he had been struck. The big gunman turned slowly, looking at Riley, then beyond him. Riley was alone.

"Hello, kid." Spooner knew what he was going to do, and he was completely at ease. "Ready to die?"

Taking a quick step, Spooner put himself behind Marie, with the girl directly in Riley's line of fire. But even as he stepped, she divined his purpose. As Spooner's hand swept down for his gun, she dropped to the floor.

Gaylord Riley felt a coldness within him, an utter stillness. He took a quick, light step to the left, putting Marie still more out of the line of fire, and as he moved, he palmed his gun and fired.

Spooner's bullet burned his neck. He felt the sharp lash of it as he fired. Hip high, his elbow at the hip, the muzzle of his gun ever so slightly turned inward toward the center of Spooner's body, he fired again.

He felt a wicked blow on his leg and it started to buckle as he fired his third shot. The bullet struck Spooner's gun, glancing upward, ripping a wide gash in his throat under his chin and ear.

Strat Spooner backed up slowly, blinking his eyes, trying to steady his gun for a final shot. He was hurt, but he had no idea how badly. Eyes wild and terrible, he tried to steady his gun for a final shot.

Riley crumpled to the floor, felt the whip of a bullet by his face and, rolling back on his elbow, he triggered his gun as fast as he could draw back the hammer. The roar of the concussions filled the room, then the hammer clicked on an empty shell. Splinters stung Riley's cheek and his eardrums went dead with the crash of a bullet into the floor alongside him.

Hurling his gun, Riley dove for Spooner's legs and brought him down in a heap. Rolling over, he saw Spooner, his face and throat covered with blood, grabbing for his eyes with rigid fingers. Striking the hands aside, Riley struck the gunman in the face with his fist, but he seemed invulnerable.

He lunged at Riley, and Riley rolled away from him, then came up to his knees. His hand swept back and grabbed the neck of the bottle behind him. He swung the bottle, a wide-arm swing with all his force, and it smashed against Spooner's skull, shattering glass.

Spooner slumped over on his face, struggled to get his hands under himself, and then, staring at Riley with wide eyes, he said, "Brazos . . . I know you now. That two-by-four kid from the Brazos!"

He got to his feet then, took two long strides, and smashed into the wall. He fell face down and rolled over and was dead.

Marie rushed to Riley and they clung to each other until a groan from the kitchen startled them. Riley attempted a step, but his leg buckled under him, and then the shock was gone and for the first time he felt weakness and pain.

Much later, when he was stretched on a bed, and Doc

Beaman had come and gone, she asked him, "What did he mean . . . about a two-by-four kid from the Brazos?"

"That's where I grew up. All of a sudden he must have remembered me from there. Seems a long time ago."

If you should come, after the passing of years, across the sagebrush levels where the lupine grows, and if by winding trails you should come to the slopes of aspen and pine, you might draw rein for a while among the columbine and mariposa lilies, and listen to the wind.

Do not look there, at the foot of the Sweet Alice Hills, for the house of Riley, for it is gone. Over the changing seasons only the hills remain the same. Yet if you should ride across the broken red lands to where the Colorado rolls, beyond Dandy Crossing you will find the trail they followed from Spanish Fork no easier.

Rimrock is gone. After the flash floods that destroyed it, only the foundations and a couple of old frame buildings remain, but higher up the hillside Ira Weaver is buried beside Dan Shattuck, who lived to see his second grandchild . . . and Sheriff Larsen, who died at ninety-two.

Kehoe married Peg Oliver, and one of their four great-grandchildren was killed in Korea on a bleak November day when, wounded and cut off from his detachment of the 27th Regiment, he settled down to show the Reds what the old breed was made of. He had eight grenades and a BAR, and twenty-three dead Chinese when he ran out of ammo.

Kehoe had been elected sheriff after Larsen retired, and Parrish had become his deputy. Parrish was killed when he interrupted a bank holdup and shot it out with two eastern gangsters. He took both of them with him when he went down shooting, and when Sampson McCarty bent over to hear his last words, Parrish said, "Jim Colburn planned 'em better!"

Colburn stayed on at the ranch as long as it operated, and then moved to Arizona. From time to time people looked him up to ask if the bad old days were really that bad, but few thought to ask about his own life. He was such a quiet-seeming man, with a shock of unruly white hair and mild blue eyes.

Gaylord Riley and Marie moved to California when the children were old enough to attend school, but the years they spent on the ranch were happy, prosperous ones.

When Senator James Colburn Riley married Blanche Kehoe they spent their honeymoon camping at the foot of the Sweet Alice Hills.

On their first night in camp their guide and packer brought a flat stone to the fireside, and Riley commented, "Looks like an old foundation stone."

"Indian, maybe," the guide said. "Nobody else in this country until around 1900. Why, outlaws didn't start usin' the Roost until about '85!"

Riley glanced at Blanche, but neither made any comment. Later, when Riley accidentally kicked an old cartridge shell out of the earth near the fire, the guide glanced at it.

"Better keep that," he said, "they don't make that kind any more."